NOIR AT A BAR
THE OXFORD FILES

FOR THE BENEFIT OF THE
OXFORD PUBLIC LIBRARY

This is a special limited edition created specifically to benefit the Oxford Public Library. Works within may have been previously published elsewhere.

Noir At A Bar and the Noir At A Bar logo are creations of Gary Zenker. He didn't invent the fedora but wears one fairly well for special occasions. Noir At A Bar has no association with anything labeled Noir At The Bar, although dem's probably good guys, too.

ISBN - 978-1-941028-33-9

White Lightning Publishing
1243 Eastwick Circle, West Chester, PA 19380

CONTENTS

And A Fistful Of Limericks by Walter Lawn and Gary Zenker

NOIR AT A BAR

STORIES OF SUSPENSE & MURDER
READ BY 10 LOCAL AUTHORS
PROCEEDS BENEFITING THE
OXFORD LIBRARY

The Oxford Library is a member of the Chester County Library System

DATE: THURSDAY, JUNE 14 - 6:30 PM UNTIL THE LAST BODY DROPS
PLACE: OCTORARA HOTEL (OTE) • 2 SOUTH THIRD STREET • OXFORD
RSVP: 610.932.9625 • OXFORDLIBRARY@CCLS.ORG • AT THE LIBRARY
TICKETS: $15 INCLUDES MEAL AND ENTERTAINMENT

INTRODUCTION

Let's just admit it: nearly everyone has the desire to kill someone at some point in their lives.

It may be the financial advisor that took off with your retirement savings, the overbearing mother-in-law who interferes in everything you do or even that bully from grade school thirty years ago. It may be the driver that cut you off while driving to work, the spouse that used the last of the toilet paper and didn't replace it, or the fast food person who once again gave you regular instead of diet soda with your combo meal.

It could be an "in the moment" thing or it can be a long-harbored feeling that doesn't really go away. There's nothing wrong with admitting it.

The healthy way to deal with it is to get it over with and just do it. Kill the offending individual. Think up a way to "off them" in the smartest, most painful way that will make them, in their final moments, regret all of the harm they ever did to you.

Well, maybe not in real life. Society tends to create laws against that and the penalties often involve sharing a cell with a guy named Bruno who is built like a tank with a tank gun to match.

Some people have resolved their darker thoughts by "using their words" in a manner very different from what their first grade teachers meant when they said it.

The results are presented on the pages before you. A number of local authors prove definitively that you really should do a background check before accepting a dinner invitation with a stranger where sharp eating utensils are involved.

These same people who would easily murder or otherwise destroy friends, relatives and even strangers show that they also have a softer side. They all volunteered to make the drive to Oxford, PA, and offer their talents for an event to raise money for the Oxford Library, a member of the Chester County Library System (they make me add that last part for reasons unknown).

The evening that became a Noir At A Bar benefit for the Oxford Public Library came from a first-time Noir At A Bar held in West Chester, PA, a joint venture between three local writers groups. We actually received a request to do it again, in Oxford. There's nothing more fun than a multiple homicide, so we said "yes."

This volume includes stories from the authors who presented their stories at Oxford Library's first-ever Noir At A Bar event, plus others who didn't present but still wanted to contribute. Each author was provided with the same basic instructions: read a story or excerpt of one you already have, or create a noir-like story for the event.

And they did. They created and read stories of suspense, crime and murder so well and with such enthusiasm that it's almost hard to imagine that these writers have very compassionate sides to them. Sarah Caine is a supporter of various animal organizations. Scott Pruden writes friendly articles on a number of community events. And Tony…well, let's just skip him by and pretend that describing how to inflict bodily damage and perfectly covering up a murder isn't his second nature. But together, these authors show their community focus as they help to raise money for the public library.

And now we also have a book to commemorate the effort. Because the writers were limited to seven-minute readings, a few submitted expanded versions of the stories they read for inclusion in this volume. So even if you heard them read their stories live, there are probably a couple of surprises here as well.

Many of these authors were doubly generous, allowing us to debut their stories here in print. Many publications will only agree to first publishing rights, so the authors gave up publishing of their stories in other more lucrative markets, once again to benefit the library.

We hope that you will enjoy these stories and seek out the other works from these authors.

Gary Zenker

AS LONG AS YOU CAN
Tony Knighton

"Hi, it's your favorite grandson."

"Who? I'm sorry, I think you've got the wrong number."

The call ends and I turn to the new guy. "That's how most of them go." I click on the arrow to call the next number. It rings and then a man says, "Hello?"

"Hi, it's your favorite grandson." The man hangs up. I try a few more and my attention wanders as I repeat the spiel. I scratch at the worn Formica tabletop. Finally, a woman says, "Charlie? It's so good to hear from you. How are you?"

I wink at the new guy and speak into the headset. "Not so good. I'm in a little trouble." As I speak I write *Charlie* on the note pad.

"Oh, no. What's wrong?"

I lean back in the swivel chair and close my eyes. "I'm down here in Florida and I did something really stupid. I was out with friends and we have this rental car, and I was driving and I was in an accident. I really didn't have that much to drink, but I got arrested."

"Oh, dear. When did this happen?"

"Just last night. Gran, I don't have enough money to get out of jail."

"Have you called your father, dear?"

I write *father* on the pad and say, "No. No, please don't tell him. Please."

This backs her up a little. "Well how can I help you, Charlie?"

I go small. "If you can send twelve hundred dollars down here I can get bailed out and nobody will have to know. Please, don't tell. He'll get really upset."

She sounds nervous. "Well – but, Charlie, I'm sure he'd understand."

"No, please. Don't tell him. Can you help me, please? I'll pay you back, I promise."

"I suppose I could. How should I send it to you?"

"You could just transfer it to my account. I just got a new one. I can give it to you now." The new guy smiles.

"Charlie, you know I don't have that kind of bank account. I'm not good with computers."

"Oh, right, right." I look at the new guy and roll my eyes. "You could go to the Western Union office and send a money order. I have the address here."

She's hesitant but says, "Let me get something to write with."

"Sure, sure." I push the microphone away from my mouth and say to the kid, "A lot of old people still don't do things on-line." He nods. I say, "Make sure you write down everything that's helpful." The lady comes back on the line; I readjust the mic and say to her, "Send it to Johnston Investigations, P.O. Box 433, Clearwater, Florida. That's the bail bondsman. Thank you so much, Gran. Dad would get really upset with me if he knew. Please, promise not to say anything to him, I'll pay you back." I end the call.

The new kid says, "Wow. That was cool."

"Thanks. Now in two days I'll call back and say 'Hi, it's Charlie.' If she's senile and doesn't remember the first call I'll just run the same line. If she does remember and asks where I am I'll tell her that there's a problem and I need more money – a lawyer, a plane ticket – whatever. It's easy. You just run this as long as you can."

"Ok. I think I got it."

"Stick to pronouns as much as possible when you're talking to them about a third party. Use the terms of familiarity carefully. It's usually ok to say 'Mom,' but watch out for 'Dad' – some fathers are 'Pop.'" He nods and I say, "What were you doing before this?"

"Phone work. Collections, mostly."

"Ok. Me, too. This is a lot like that. Just a different affect. Try to sound young and scared. You'll get the hang of it."

I go back to my spot, past the others working phone lines set up on folding tables. I overhear snatches of conversations like the one I've just had as I sit down and settle in. Angela, the girl next to me, says over her headset, "Oh, that sounds really darling." She smiles at me and continues, "I can't wait to see it."

She must be working a follow up call. Angela's good. She has a great ear. All of us can adjust our speech to match the mark's; in fact most people do this unconsciously, like the way you find yourself saying "aye" if you talk long enough with an off-the-boat Irishman. Angela's got more than that. For this call she's doing a rural twang that puts me in mind of one of the western states – Wyoming or Montana – she's probably working a chump who lives somewhere along the I-90 corridor. I watch her a few moments more. Even under the fluorescent lights her face is pretty – she has these really beautiful green eyes – but she needs to lose about a hundred pounds and she probably never will.

I get back to work and make calls until seven in the evening. I log off and stand. I've been sitting too long; my ankle is stiff. I walk over to Steve's desk. Without looking up he says, "What's up?"

"I'm taking off. What do you have for me?" Steve opens the cabinet behind him and fishes out an envelope. I take it; it feels thin. "I need to talk to Mr. Josef."

"Everybody needs to talk to Mr. Josef. What about?"

I hold up the envelope. "I need to make more money."

"Then make more calls."

"Look, I want to talk—"

"I'll tell him. Anything else?"

I can tell that he's tired of this conversation. "No." There's nothing to be gained by talking to Steve anyway. I leave. Down the stairs, out the door and onto Noble Street – hardly more than an alley. I go a dozen steps and hear the door open behind me. It's Angela. She calls to me in her own voice, "Hank, wait a minute."

I stop and turn. It's sad; she's been waiting for me to leave. I give her a smile and say, "Hey. What's up?"

She catches up and we walk together. We turn south onto 11th Street, toward Chinatown. She says, "I don't know. Do you want to get something to eat?"

There's a part of me that likes her. She's smart and she's talented – one of the top earners in the room – and she's funny. All she wants is to feel wanted, which is why another part of me hates her – she makes me hate myself, forces me to acknowledge just how shallow I am.

Even now, walking along the sidewalk with her I find myself maintaining distance – staying apart from her, far enough away to keep anyone from thinking that I'm with her. As if anyone would even care. The worst is that I know that she knows; she's in the game, she reads body language as well as I do. I say, "No thanks. I'm gonna go home and turn in. I'm beat."

She tries once more. "Why don't you come over and stay at my place. We wouldn't have to do anything."

Her naked display of feelings is tough to watch. I cut it short. "I don't think so. Not tonight."

She tries to smile, and says, "Sure. Some other time," and turns and walks back the way we came.

I grab a *City Paper* from the box in front of the noodle place on the next corner and read it at my table while I wait for my order. I drink two beers along with the bowl of green curry and walk home. I'm on the fifth floor of a Chinese supermarket, in the middle of a row of four and five story buildings. It's a one hundred year-old brick and joist monstrosity with a peeling sign hung over the display windows. Above that a ratty-looking fire escape is bolted to the facade. You can smell dried fish all through the place, but like anything else, you get used to it.

An ancient Otis Elevator services all five floors. The first two are the store; meat, fish and produce on the first floor, canned and dry goods on the second. The basement is storage. The top three floors are given over to apartments; there must be three-dozen people in the rooms below me, mostly new arrivals from various Asian shit holes. I have the fifth floor to myself. It's mostly an open loft with the actual living space in one corner. An artist had the place before me and used it to do silk screens. The rest of the people in the building must think I'm Genghis Khan or something.

Inside, I open Steve's envelope and count; there are eleven one hundred dollar bills inside. I get my book out of the dresser drawer and calculate. Even with what Mr. Josef is deducting, I should have more.

I go to the kitchen and pry off the backsplash with a table knife; I take out the fireproof box I keep wedged into the pipe chase and add the hundreds less three to the money in the box, and replace it.

For the time being I belong to Mr. Josef. I took from him and he's taking back. He gets these lists of senior citizens – people making Medicare payments to doctor's offices, people with reverse mortgages – then he sets up a boiler room and gets people like me and Angela to work the phones. I would be making decent coin if not for the penance I was paying.

I've found an angle, though, a way to tap into the list and my own drop. I call a few of the numbers and try my spiel. The first three get me nothing, and then a woman says, "Is that you, Sonny?"

I write *Sonny* on a pad of paper along with the number and say, "Yes, it is. How are you?"

"I'm happy to hear from you. When are you coming to see me?" She has an upper-class voice; there's a flute-like tone in her speech.

"Well that's kind of why I'm calling. I have a problem."

"What is it, dear?"

I start to walk around the apartment as I talk. "I'm embarrassed to say." I like it better here, on my own, than cooped up in a chair at a table on Noble Street.

"Sonny, you can tell me anything. I'm your grandmother."

I wait a moment and say, "You can't tell anyone about this."

"What, baby?"

"I'm in jail."

That takes the breath out of her. "Sonny, what happened?"

"I'm in Boston. I was out with friends—"

"Friends from college?"

"Yes," I write that down and say, "yes. I didn't have that much to drink but I got in a little accident on the way back to the airport and the other driver went to the hospital."

"Oh, dear."

"I know." I let it sit for a moment and then say, "I don't have enough money to post bail."

"How much do you need?" Worried.

"Bail has been set at fifty thousand." I hear her take in a breath and I say, "If you can send me ten percent a bondsman will post the rest."

"I can't put my hands on that much money tonight, sweetheart. I wish you'd let me talk to your father."

I wander to the front window and watch traffic on the street through the iron grating of the fire escape. "No. Please don't do that. He'll just go crazy."

"Now, Sonny, I'm sure—"

I go out on a limb. "He didn't tell you about the last time, did he?"

"No. What do you mean, the last time?"

"It doesn't matter. He'll be really angry." I take another chance. "That's all right. I understand. It's a lot of money. It's too much."

"No, Sonny. I'll go to the bank tomorrow and wire the funds." She pauses and then says, "Where shall I send it?"

I give her the address and say, "Thank you so much. Please, please don't tell father. He'll go crazy."

"No. Don't worry. I won't speak a word of this to anyone. I'll wire the funds in the morning." She hesitates and then says, "I love you."

"I love you too, Gran. I've got to go now—"

"No, please, talk to me a bit longer. I miss you so much." It sounds like she's starting to cry. "It's been so long since I've seen you. I miss your visits."

"I know, Gran, but they won't let me tie up the phone much longer. I really have to go."

"All right, Sonny. I love you with all my heart."

I hang up and look out the window; it's early but I'm not in the mood for any more calls. I shut off the lights and go back out.

I walk into Center City. There's a fair number of people on the streets for a weekday night and my mood improves. I go into a yuppie joint called Misconduct and take a seat at the bar between two suits. The one to the left of me is talking shop with the guy on his far side. The other is alone, watching the Phillies pitcher try to work his way out of bases loaded.

I put a twenty on the bar and ask the guy what the score is. He's got money on the bar and a set of keys that includes one for a Saab. We talk up the game and I order a beer and buy him one, too. The pitcher walks in a run but strikes out the next batter to end the inning, and a commercial for on-line insurance comes onto the screen. The guy next to me buys a round and tells me that he's a mortgage broker. I give him some line of bull about bonds and in their next at-bats the Phils go down one, two, three. The guy gets up to go to the bathroom. I finish my beer and palm his keys.

Outside I get lucky; he was parked in the lot just down the block. I drive downtown to South Philly and haggle with the guy at the chop shop on Emily Street; we settle on twenty-eight hundred for the car.

I stop into a hipster place on Passyunk Avenue and have a few more beers but can't really get anything going. It's late and I'm a little bit drunk. I take out my phone and tap Angela's number. It rings and then she says, "Hi, Hank." She sounds subdued.

"Angela, hi. I was wondering if I could take you up on that offer to come over."

She waits a moment and then says, "It's late, Hank. I don't know."

"Sure, sure. That's ok. I didn't realize how late it was. I'm sorry if I woke you."

"That's all right. I haven't been asleep."

"Oh. Well if you're busy—"

"No. I was, earlier, but not now." We're both quiet and then she says. "Come on over. It's ok."

I cab over. She lives in an apartment above a nail salon, in the middle of an unbroken row of two story buildings. She buzzes me in. Her door is ajar. She's in her living room, wearing pajamas and a robe. "Angela, I'm sorry. You were asleep when I called."

She lies, "No, I wasn't. I like to get comfy when I come home, that's all. Can I get you a drink?" She comes up to me and puts her hand on my cheek.

"No thanks."

Later on, as we stare at the bedroom ceiling she asks me, "How long are you going to do this, Hank?"

This question is loaded. I say, "What do you mean?" I don't want to do this – I think she wants to talk about our "relationship.'

But I'm wrong. She says, "You know. Make phone calls. How long?"

I relax and say, "Long enough to pay off Mr. Josef. After that I don't know. I might hang with him for a while if he starts paying me decently."

"I don't mean that. I mean the life. Don't you ever think of getting out, doing something straight?"

"No. I've been in the life since the day I was born."

That's not really accurate. I'd been in this before I was born. My mother learned that she was pregnant during her entry physical at Muncie. She was two months along and figured that carrying me to term would mean a softer job and maybe better food. If not for prison, I wouldn't have been along for the ride.

She was doing a ten-year stretch for second degree murder. She and a hard guy had been running a badger scheme. He knocked a man out; the man never woke up.

Mom had me in the prison infirmary and I ended up going to her mother. Granny hadn't been overjoyed but she made the most of it. She liked stores. She'd wheel me along with her while she shopped. I was better than any booster bag; lots of nice things made the ride out the door under my blankets. When I got too big for a stroller, she taught me to pitch a fit. I was great; I'd end up on my back on some department store floor, screaming, arms and legs going. It was something to see. In fact, people couldn't help watching. Granny would take the opportunity to pick up some more nice things. As I got more wise, I would pretend to be lost. I learned a lot from Granny.

It wasn't until I went to school that I saw what I was missing. Most of the other kids lived in houses, had a family, played games, sports. They weren't on any hustle. The first time I went to another kid's house after school was the first time I saw how straight people lived. It was like going to Mars. I went upstairs to the bathroom and then found his parent's bedroom and palmed a pair of his mother's earrings.

Angela is asleep as I get dressed and let myself out. The bars are closed and the streets empty save a straggler here and there. I turn up Seventh Street and see two bike cops slow to look me over. I walk toward them and say, "Have you seen a little dog?" I use my hands to show how big. "She's a mutt, mostly black."

The cops shake their heads. One says, "Sorry."

"Her name's Sugar. If you do see her." They ride on, and I walk home and go to bed.

In the morning I pick up coffee on the way to work. Angela's not there. I make a few calls and then Mr. Josef comes in with the two hard guys that follow him around. They're both tall and lean. Frightening. One has a shaved head and a neck tat. The other has some hair on his head but it's buzzed – I'd guess a #2 clipper, neither of these guys are brains but neither are dumb enough to give somebody something to grab onto. They wear two rings apiece on the fingers of either hand. Both were boxers who Mr. Josef had a piece of once; now they work for him outright. I don't know their names. They don't talk much.

Mr. Josef is different—he likes to talk. For a thug, he doesn't seem too bad a guy. He is a thug, though. People assume that he's a Russian, but he's not; he's a YAC – that stands for Yugoslavia, Albania, and Croatia, countries that sit along the Adriatic, the western terminus of the old Silk Road. Mr. Josef has the high cheekbones and dark eyes that hint of Mongol ancestry.

He came here in the early nineties during the Eastern European criminal exodus after the Soviet empire collapsed. Real wild men. They made a big splash here on the east coast when they first came over, playing the old games by new rules. They mechanized burglary – cutting through store roofs or security grates with gasoline-powered circular saws, or pulling ATMs out of convenience stores with a winch – right through the display windows. Smash and grab on steroids. These were people who belonged to ethnic groups largely excluded from the legitimate economy where they came from, so what else were they going to do once they got here?

Sprees like theirs never last long though; a lot of them went to jail. Most didn't care. One time Mr. Josef rolled up his sleeve and showed me a gang tattoo from the old world, a two-headed bird of prey. "After what I've seen, American prison sounds like country club." He rolled his sleeve back down. "We sometimes had to fight for food." He doesn't miss many meals lately. You would still have to describe him as muscular instead of fat, but he's on his way. The top three buttons of his black silk shirt are open and reveal his joke, a small gold Star of David on a chain nesting in his gray chest hair. He's not a Jew; he got here by falsely claiming to be one seeking asylum.

He talks to Steve for a minute. As he makes to leave I say, "Mr. Josef, could I have a minute of your time?"

He looks at his Rolex and says, "Today is not good. Already, I am late." He smiles and says, "Patience. Patience in all things." He stops smiling and continues, "Only thing more important is loyalty." I don't like how he looks at me or how it feels; I turn away from his stare. As they move toward the door the hard guys sneer at me.

Angela walks in as they are leaving. As always, Mr. Josef makes a fuss over her. "There she is. There is my princess."

Angela blushes and says, "Hello, Mr. Josef."

He gives her a peck on the cheek and steps back. "If I was twenty years younger, I would run away with you, princess. Thanks to you again for the help you are giving."

She sits down next to me and starts the laptop in front of her. She's too much of a sport to say anything like *what happened to you last night? I missed you.* She just says, "Hi, Hank," and goes to work.

My grandmother's boyfriend Buddy got me into the telephone business. "Work smarter, not harder," he'd say. The first job I did with him was an out and out scam – collecting for fireman's widows. "Everybody likes the firemen and everybody feels bad for their old ladies." My voice had changed early and it turned out that I was a natural; I could put just the right note of pathos into the spiel that would tug at the heartstrings and open the chump's wallets. Buddy coached me – taught me the fine points of the life. "Try to do as much as you can by yourself. Partners are undependable. A grifter's gotta grift, and he'll take you if he can. If you need to team up with somebody, watch them like a hawk."

This was all before computers, before on-line transfers, before Kickstarter and Paypal. You needed to have a physical drop – a real address or a post office box – so you were always running around, changing things. The postal inspectors finally caught up with Bud.

After he went away I worked a few boiler rooms but the problem with working for crooks is just that – you're working for crooks. Much of the time they were bad pay or no pay at all.

I found the collection business by accident; I answered an ad in the *Philadelphia Weekly* and went to work the next night. I'd thought it would be just another con game, but it wasn't, it was calling deadbeats, collecting on past-due bills. It didn't take me long to figure the angles and when I put some cash together I bought my own package of bad debt from a skip tracer for six cents on the dollar. I worked the paper on my own and doubled a five K investment in four days, then turned around and sold the leftover paper to another operator for thirty-five hundred. The best part of the whole thing was that it was legit, or at least mostly legit. Granny was pleased when I visited her in the home. You'd have thought I'd just gone to work for NASA. "I'm really proud of you, Hank. I always knew you'd do good."

I kept on doing good. I hooked up with an Asian guy named Kim, a techie who showed me how to piggyback other operator's lists – essentially steal their paper. He set up the drops too, so all I had to do was make the calls. Our overhead was next to nothing. It was all good until the day that the two hard guys stopped me in the street and took me to see Mr. Josef. The only reason I lived through the visit was he knew that I could make money for him. He laid it out: I would hand over the money I had on hand and go to work for him until I had satisfied my debt. They pressed me for Kim; they threw me down a flight of stairs. Broke my ankle in two places. I was really scared but I wouldn't give him up. Mr. Josef respected that. He thought it showed loyalty. I'd just thought they'd kill me once I'd told.

Angela leaves before I do. I work another hour and go home, riding the noisy elevator to my floor. I log on and check on the drop – it's an account that Kim set up. The five thousand dollars from the call last night is there. Tomorrow I'll turn it into cash and talk to Kim. I look around the kitchen and decide that I'm not hungry so I call a few more numbers on the list. I get no play. Even though I know that it's too soon, I call the old lady from last night. "Hi, this is Sonny."

"I've been thinking about you all day. Is everything all right now?"

"Well, no. I still have a problem."

She's upset. "Didn't you get the money, dear?"

"Oh, yes, I got the money. Thank you very much."

"Then what's wrong?"

"Well, this is sort of embarrassing."

"Go on, Sonny. You know that you can tell me anything."

"I got into a fight. Here at the police station."

"Oh, dear. Are you all right?"

"Yes, yes, I'm all right. But I hurt the fellow I had the trouble with and now I'm being charged with assault, too."

"Sonny, that doesn't sound like you."

"You're right. It's not me. I couldn't help it. I need more money to make bail, seven thousand. Can you help me again? Please?"

"That's an awful lot of money. I don't know."

"Please. I hate to ask you again but I can't ask anyone else. Dad would go nuts."

"All right, Sonny. I'll do it." I could hear her start to choke up. "I love you so much." She sobs and then says, "Please stop this. It's not the real you."

I hesitate and then say, "You're right. I'll never do this again. Thank you. I have to go now."

" No, not yet, please. I don't think you have any idea what you mean to me, Sonny."

"Sure I do, Gran. I love you, too."

"No. I don't think you really know. I, I'd do anything for you."

The woman is starting to choke up and I want the call to end. I say, "I have to go. I'll see you soon," and hang up.

I get a bowl of hot and sour soup at the place on the corner and then cab up to Fairmount. I meet a girl named Nikki at the London. She has long black hair and long legs and I chat her up over drinks. We end up going to a party at her girlfriend's house in Brewerytown where we dance. When the party winds down I go with her to her place. She offers me some blow and we do a few lines. I won't turn down a toot now and then but I'm not really into drugs, and I definitely won't deal – way too much trouble. Sooner or later all those guys do time and that's not me, never have, never will. Later, as I leave Nikki's apartment I check my phone and see that Angela has sent me a text: *I had fun with you last night.*

Mom didn't keep in touch once she got out. It's never bothered me much; the only times we had together were upstate, in the visitors' room. She'd say hi! and how is school? but she'd mostly talk to Granny, thank her for the cigarettes and ask what was new.

Granny passed away last year. I kind of thought that Mom might show up for the service. Only a few people did, old timers that I didn't know. I told the mortician to keep the ashes.

Angela is at her spot when I get to work. She looks like she's been crying but asking would mean negotiating a minefield. I just say hello.

She speaks softly. "Do you ever just hate things so much that you want to run away?"

I have thought of running. Mr. Josef scared me yesterday. But this is tricky, talking to Angela, talking to her here. I'm careful. I say, "Sometimes. But then, where would I go? One place is pretty much like any another."

She doesn't look at me, she just says, "I think if I have to come in here one more time and look at these four walls I'll explode. Don't you hate it here?"

I've never thought about this at all; this just happens to be where I work. For the sake of her feelings, I hedge. "I'm not nuts about the décor, but the color of the walls isn't as important as the color of the money."

She doesn't laugh. She bites her bottom lip and looks at the floor. She says, "I'm getting out of here. I'm leaving." There are tears in her eyes. "Would you come with me? I'll go wherever you want. Would you, Hank?"

"Angela, I can't go anywhere. I owe Mr. Josef." I move to put my arm around her but stop, conscious of myself. I hear the conversations in the room slow and then stop altogether. The other callers are watching us. "Look, let's go outside and talk."

"No." She shakes her head and stands, says, "no thank you," gathers her things and leaves.

After work I visit Kim at his loft. There's more gear than furniture in his place; most of it is a mystery to me. He's listening to some Asian-trash remix. I ask him to lower the volume and then say, "Mr. Josef said some things to me yesterday that make me uneasy. Are you being careful?"

"Always, Hank. I don't need any trouble from the Russian mob."

"Nobody does. But I got the distinct impression from him that he smells something fishy." I let Kim chew on that and then say, "You and me are the only two that know what we're doing, right?"

"Of course, baby. Why would I spoil a good thing?"

I'm not sure. I nod and put his share of our earnings on his worktable. He says, "Oh, Merry Christmas to me," as he thumbs through the bills. He looks up at me and says, "We need to talk about finances. I want a bigger cut from now on."

"Why?" I motion to the hardware strewn about the loft, "Don't you have enough toys?"

"Sure I do, but I always want more." He chuckles and stands. "Look, Economics 101. Supply and demand. There aren't many guys around that do what I do. On the other hand, there are a lot of guys that I can get to do what you do."

I push back. "You've been doing really well with me." I get more nervous as I think about the angles. Could Josef have found him? I keep talking just to try and see how much he might have given away. "I'm the one who has to put the time in."

He doesn't bite. Smiling, he says, "I don't care. You're in no position to argue with me about this. The drop," he points at his laptop, "is in another galaxy now. I put it somewhere you'll never find without me. So don't argue anymore, just say yes and get out of here."

So the old lady's seven thousand is gone now. I tell myself not to get mad. This is how things go sometimes. I leave Kim's without saying anything.

The wind picks up as I walk home. It's almost chilly. I get less angry and more worried about Mr. Josef. Has Kim thrown me under the bus? I decide while I'm walking home that it's time to cut and run. I'm frightened. By the time I get to my building I'm paranoid: I'm sure that Kim called Mr. Josef, sure that someone is waiting for me in my apartment. I take the steps instead of the noisy elevator. I'm breathing hard as I climb the last flight. I sneak a look. There's no one in the hall. I put my ear to the door and wait. Then I ease my key into the lock and turn it as slowly as I can manage and ease the door open. No one is inside. My pulse slows and I put some clothes and things I'll need in a bag and then pry open the backsplash. The money's there and I throw it into the bag with everything else.

As I'm making my way through the apartment to see if I've left anything, I notice the pad of paper on the dining room table and I think about the old lady. She's good for one more touch. I could go to Boston tonight and set up an old school drop at the Western Union office. I take out the burner and punch in her numbers.

"Hello?"

"Grandmother, it's me, Sonny."

"Sonny, is everything all right?"

"Not yet. There was some problem at my arraignment. I only had a public defender and he messed something up. I don't really understand what happened."

She says, "Oh, no." She sounds defeated. Rich people have a hard time when life doesn't work the way they expect.

I press. "One of the cops has been really nice to me. He knows a lawyer that can get me out by tomorrow."

She sighs and asks, "How much money will he need?"

I smile now and say, "He's kind of expensive. He needs a ten thousand dollar retainer, but that takes care of everything else that comes down in the case."

I can hear that she's starting to tear up. She says, "Hold on a moment, dear," and puts down the phone. I can hear her speaking with someone, muffled, and then she's back on the line. "I love you very much but I can't do this anymore." She sounds like she's crying.

"Gran, please, I know that it's a lot of money but I swear, I'll pay you back. I have to get out of here."

She blows her nose and says, "You're not going anywhere, Hank."

I recognize her voice and almost piss myself. I look out the window; Mr. Josef has pulled up in his El Dorado. The hard guys get out and walk toward my building. For the first time in my life I'm speechless.

Angela continues, "Mr. Josef knew someone was stealing his numbers. He put some traps onto the list. I knew it was you the first time you called, Hank. Mr. Josef trusted me and I didn't tell him. Why didn't you just stop?" I hear the front door go. "It kills me. Every day. Sitting there next to you, knowing the best thing that I can hope for is that maybe you'll come by in the middle of the night."

I hear the elevator car creaking its way up the shaft. It'll be carrying one of them; the other will take the stairs. Mr. Josef will only get out of the car if I'm stupid enough to try the fire escape. I look at the phone in my hand and end the call.

Originally published in
Happy Hour and Other Philadelphia Cruelties
Crime Wave Press in 2015

A DARK STORMY NIGHT

'Twas a dark stormy night in Sin City.

At the end of the bar, she looked pretty.

Her gat did him in

Ere he'd finished his gin

His tab was paid up, more's the pity.

STATUTE OF LIMITATIONS
Gary Zenker

"Debt?" I asked.

"Four to ten years, depending on the state," she replied.

"Taxes?"

"Federal – three years following filing of the return. Six, if they determine fraud."

"Sexual misconduct?"

"Look at the news recently with Cosby and Weinstein. Apparently none."

"Murder?"

"No limit. They can come for you at any time." She interrupted her own rambling. "So who?"

"It's just a theoretical."

She stared me directly in the eyes. "I know you. You don't KNOW how to do theoretical."

I bit at the cuticle of my right thumb, then spit a small piece of skin onto the floor.

"As your attorney…" she began…

"As my attorney, you are bound by lawyer-client privilege," I finished for her.

"*Only* if you come for my representation *afterwards*. *Not* if I know about the crime ahead of time. And certainly *not* if it's a capital offense." She cited some legal bruhaha I didn't care about. "You can't rely on spousal protection, you know." Spouses can't be forced to testify against each other. But we aren't married any more.

We had an amicable divorce five years prior, at MY instigation. That is, if you can consider being forced to give your ex- seven-eighths of everything you own with the exception of a classic Gibson Guitar collection, to be amicable. I am sure that her having to win at everything is a terrible burden for her...almost as much as it was for me. I'm not sure which she hated worse: my filing for divorce or her inability to clean me out entirely. But I did win my freedom. Well, if you can believe living in a one-bedroom efficiency and struggling to pay my rent each month, to be a win.

It improved our relationship. We could now sit in the same room together without arguing about virtually everything. And once every two weeks or so, we now grab cocktails and dinner, then hump like animals no matter who either of us may be dating at the time. It's strange how a divorce and a forced colonoscopy can make someone more attractive. She still makes me pay for the dinner, of course.

"What's your motivation....money? Revenge? Love?" She emphasized that last word like one teenager goading another. I didn't respond. "Ah, it's love then." She nodded and her lips curled to what appeared to be her version of a tight smile. "So let's see. She's otherwise involved. Maybe married...probably married. You need a clean path. The husband has money. You aren't doing it for that, but it would be a nice bonus. You could use it and she would lose it in the divorce." This is why she is the lawyer and I am living where I am.

"So you need a plan. An alibi. And maybe a defense in case the alibi isn't enough. Of course, I'm not really having this discussion with you so…"

There's nothing like a lawyer to help you plan out your next illegal act: they are the masters of loopholes. Suddenly, our dinner has become a business meeting, and I expect a bill much larger than the dinner check is coming my way. Lawyers don't offer anyone a friends and family discount, especially to ex's.

Two hours later, I have a plan better than I ever could have thought up myself, with all the angles covered. I have a plan, an alibi and a smart lawyer in my corner.

A week later, I'm with Betty and her soon-to-be-deceased husband in an expensive hotel suite in a city hours from where they live together. A business trip for him slash romantic surprise from her slash murder opportunity for me. It's cliché but I watch from the closet. One more sip and two more minutes, and he'll collapse to the floor. Five more minutes and his breathing will stop completely. The trick that the ex- taught me wasn't to hide the cause of death but rather point the blame in a different direction. It works in the courtroom all the time, she assured me.

As I emerge from the closet, she kisses my cheek. I flip open the top of a medicine bottle and jiggle two pills onto the floor and kick them under the dresser, to give the detectives a reward for their detailed examination of the room. He'll be discovered by housekeeping tomorrow, dead and wallet-less. Toxicology will show high levels of drugs in his system, matching the pills they found. The obvious suspect will be a mystery woman from a discreet out-of-town encounter while on business. Another cheating husband on a business trip. Not original but entirely believable.

Before we leave, his beautiful widow will go home to play the confused spouse when the police visit to inform her of the murder. But it's a shame to waste the untainted champagne, so she and I take a moment to celebrate with clean glasses. We'll take them with us and dump them in a can at a convenience store between here and home. It's all so perfectly planned. We toast and drink.

Suddenly, I can't keep my balance. The room starts spinning, and speeds up quickly. I drop the bottle and glass, then fall to my knees. My love falls beside me. I'm paralyzed but still conscious. My ex- exits from the bathroom and appears over me, smiling. She was hiding here before me? Too many damn hiding places in this luxury suite. My head spins.

Our perfect plan.

Her perfect plan.

I poison the hubby, and then his wife (my new woman) and I "accidentally" poison each other. All wrapped neatly in a bow for the police.

"I hate when there's anything still left on the table," she says from above. I can't be sure if she's referring to the champagne or my collection. As my executor, I'm sure she'll figure a way get the guitars after all.

Statutes of limitations. I forgot the most important one. A woman scorned. Apparently, there's no time limits on that one, either.

VERONICA BROWN

A dame named Veronica Brown

Wore a deeply revealing red gown.

But it did hide her feckless

Hostess' diamond necklace.

Now Veronica's moving uptown.

TEN ORGANS YOU DON'T WANT TO LOSE IN A BAR FIGHT

Tony Conaway

"You're asking for a list?"

"Yah. Say you're in a bar fight, and you're going to lose an organ or two. Which ones?" We were, of course, sitting in a bar: me, Moose and Colin.

"Easy-peasy," said Moose. "I –"

"And you can't say your reproductive organs." Colin waved off Moose's objections. "Too easy."

"Shit. Those are the only ones I really use." Moose rose unsteadily and lurched towards the men's room.

"Just organs, or do glands count, too? 'cause I think you can lose your thyroid or pituitary glands."

"Whatever. If you got 'em, which ones can't you loose. Lose." Colin had been drinking two shots to my one. He must've been hammered.

"OK. Let's start with the ones you CAN lose: spleen, gallbladder, appendix. People have those removed all the time, and they do just fine."

"Can't see how you'd lose your appendix in a bar fight. Nor gallbladder neither. Spleen, sure. A bad impact and they gotta cut it out. Happens in contact sports all the time."

"Yeah, but 'bar fight' is pretty nebulous. The guy could have a knife, a broken bottle, even an icepick. You get punctured in the right place, and it's good-bye, gallbladder."

"OK. Knives but no guns. Which organs DON'T you want to lose?"

"Well, none you need to survive: brain, heart, lungs…pancreas. Both kidneys."

Colin was counting off with his fingers – but on the hand where he'd lost his pinky. He switched to his other hand. "That's five. What else?"

"Skin!" came a voice from below. "Biggest organ you losers've got! Not me, though."

We both looked over the table. Moose hadn't made it to the men's room. He was lying on the floor. He'd also used another organ: his bladder. There were two empty chairs at our table; Colin and I put our feet up on the seats to keep them out of the spreading puddle of urine.

"I don't see how you could lose all your skin in a bar fight," Colin said.

"No one even scalps anybody anymore," I said.

"To the lost art of scalping!" We clinked glasses and downed our shots. Then I refilled our glasses from the bottle, because, why not?

"If we include glands, you can lose your tonsils and adenoids. I had mine taken out when I was a kid."

Colin shook his head. "If someone can reach inside and down your throat to remove your tonsils in a bar fight, they belong on 'America's Got Talent,' not…." He didn't seem to know how to finish that sentence.

"He'd need a lil' baby arm to fit in your mouth 'n' reach down your throat," Moose said from the floor.

I didn't even want to think about some killer baby reaching inside my mouth.

"Moving on," I said. "You want to keep fighting, you need your eyes. And your ears." At the moment, ears were on my mind, since I couldn't seem to hear out of my left one. "You can live without your nose, but I got mine broke once in a fight and it hurt so bad I couldn't even see. Can't fight blind. Sense of taste, I suppose I could do without."

"Nothing tastes right anymore," Colin said. "Not even this scotch."

I was pretty sure we were drinking bourbon, but I didn't bother to point that out.

That reminded me. "Stomach! That's an organ. Don't want to lose that."

"To eat with?" Colin asked. I heard sirens approaching. Cops.

"To drink with!" We lifted our glasses to toast again. My glass kind of stuck to the table. I realized that the blood from Colin's severed pinky had spread across the tabletop. Or maybe it was blood from the stump of my left ear.

"Guess it's time," Colin said. Now the police were at the door, screaming at us to raise our hands and get on the floor. As if I'd get on the floor, wet with the blood of the guys we'd killed! And Moose's piss. I noticed that Moose hadn't said anything for a while – he was probably dead of his wounds, too.

"Go out with a bang?" I asked.

"Only way to go," said Colin.

We didn't even manage to get our guns out before the cops shot us down.

This story originally appeared in
Near To The Knuckle

THIS BOOK IS TO DIE FOR
Matthew McGeehin

My mother told me murder is very much like a library: you should keep quiet about it. She was assassinated when I was thirteen. Strange, strange woman. But I always remembered it when I poured over the thick volumes on the bookshelf that made up one wall of my office. I said I'd make time to read them about twelve years ago, and now I was wondering whether or not I should donate them. Fill the shelf up with something useful, like whiskey. That way, if they aged from neglect, they'd get better.

But I never did it. It was the only memento I had left of her. Even if it was only because she told me her little ditty every time she saw me read. Was a stupid thing to dwell on, she'd been gone for a while. But there wasn't much else to do when I waited. I'd grabbed a thick one and gotten fairly interested, but I kept my mind on my clock. I had a meeting scheduled. For fifteen minutes ago. How rude. Why did I set the meeting for today? I was still getting over that tetch of the flu I had, so much I was wearing one of those face masks. I was pretty sure the doctor made me wear it so I'd feel guilty about shifting it to the side to get in my normal daydrinking. Well, he didn't know me that well. I was already on my fifth.

After another minute, the door opened. In she stepped, all hips, dressed in a slinky red number that screamed "I am trouble, I will probably kill you. But you'll like it when I do." Just who I was looking for.

"I thought you PI types had secretaries." She paced across the room, tracing one of her elegant fingers across the bookshelves.

I pointed to my face mask. "Supposed to limit contact with people. Pretty sure OSHA wouldn't be pleased if I was infecting my staff."

"What does that say for me, then?"

"You wanted to wait?" I cocked an eyebrow. And there was a slight smile from her. No, she wouldn't. She couldn't. Neither could I. "I'd still keep my distance. No contagion."

She only smiled for a second. "Where is it?"

"So soon? And we were just getting to know each other."

"I learned the hard way not to mix business with pleasure."

"What are those hips, then?"

"Something I'm throwing in for free."

I stared. "Where's my money?" She had her lessons, I learned mine. Always get what you wanted first.

"Where's my intel? I don't pay you for nothing."

I shrugged. So that's how it was going to be. "Over there." I pointed towards the bookshelf. "You're looking for *The Tempest.*" She again traced her fingers across the shelf.

"Why is this so dusty?"

"Because I don't want to clean it. Also, it prevents people from searching there. No one looks in a dusty corner for valuables." Miss Trouble sneezed in response, but eventually, pulled the thick book from the shelf.

As she did so, it nearly fell to the floor. "This is really heavy."

"That way, no one can steal it." I smiled behind my mask. She attempted to open the cover, and I laughed as she failed. "Not one for high literature, are you?" I laughed to myself. "It's one of those book safes. There's a trick to opening it. I'll tell you when you pay me."

She laughed only slightly. Then she reached into her purse. I tried to look shocked when she pulled a Saturday Night Special on me. In this business, you grew to expect that.

She leveled the gun at my brain. Rude, I was using that. Sometimes. "You knew this was coming. Tell me how to open it. Now." Her voice was deathly calm. What was the world coming too? Shooting a man in his office just before lunch? Murder was supposed to be just after breakfast or after leaving a bar. Like civilized people do it.

"Push the three 'T's." She followed my instructions without taking her eyes off me. I could hear the slight click from the book. Eagerly, Miss Trouble pulled it open, only to wince and drop the book right on my desk. There was nothing inside but a little prank I rigged up with an airgun. Blew the cloud of dust right in her eyes.

"Was this this joke?" She had no sense of humor. Her eyes were nearly pink with irritation. She wiped them with her arm, but I knew she'd try that. It would just make it worse.

"You think I would tell you where it is? It's not even here. I knew how this was going to end. And I prepared for it."

She growled again, raised the gun, in time enough to hear police sirens wailing in the distance. Her face turned white, and she turned back to me. I grabbed the book I'd been reading from my desk and blocked my head with it, but I felt the bullet shoot me right in my chest. I fell to the floor as I heard her bolt from the room.

After about five minutes, I stood up and felt the impact of her bullet on my bulletproof vest. Knew she wouldn't aim for the face once things got crazy, she was a terrible shot even at close range. And between the sounding sirens and the irritation in her eyes, she wouldn't waste time lining one up.

I turned off the tape recorder hidden under the desk, and the sounds of the sirens stopped. It was so easy to hit it with my toe while Miss Trouble was fiddling with the safe.

I stepped out of the office and went to my car. The bulletproof vest saved my life, but I was still pretty sore from the shot. Thoughts of nursing the aches with a shot of Jack, or several, flitted through my mind, but I wrote it off. I had a ship to catch. A cruise, no less. One week away from the grime and sleaze of the city and the job. Trench coats and whiskey shots would be replaced with board shorts and fruity umbrella drinks.

I'd earned it. I needed it too, and not just because I'd been shot. Getting away for a week would prevent Miss Trouble from finding out that reports of my death were greatly exaggerated. Plus, she'd need the time too. That dust in her eye looked like it really stung.

A week would be long enough for the ricin to do its work. Rubbing it into her eyes like she did, it was like she'd forgotten how such poisons worked. I didn't keep the face mask on just because of the flu, it protected me from any cross-contamination.

I wonder if she'd realize it was the same poison she used to kill my mother, all those years ago. Probably not. For Miss

Trouble, my mother's death was just a loose end. She wouldn't have known there was a little boy who watched his mother die, with everyone powerless to save her. Maybe she'd find out, just before the end. Maybe she'd remember. Maybe it would make a good story.

But then I remembered what Mother said about libraries, and figured I'd keep it to myself.

CAUGHT

She was caught with a gun in her hand.

The guy had bled out in the sand.

"It's not me," she exclaimed.

"It's another," she blamed.

"The Beach Butler has done it again."

OVERDUE

Joanette McGeoch

It was a dark and stormy night! Nah, just kidding.

Really, it was a bright and sunny day in the middle of summer. Hot actually. With little wisps of white fluffy clouds drifting by. But Julia was in a dark and stormy mood. With her bare feet up on the table, sitting on her back porch looking out onto the flower garden, she was thinking deep. Her white shorts that snuggly fit her young firm body rode up her thighs as she nervously tapped her crossed ankles flashing hot pink nail polish.

The wild white roses that climbed profusely over the porch rail released a light sweet scent in the silken breeze.

She took a long, hard drink from the glass on the table. The ice cubes rattled and a few drops of wet moisture fell on her thigh. She took the glass from her lips and put it back down on the table. Lemonade was her drink of choice. She liked it bitter and straight with lots of rind. She looked like a sweet librarian with long blonde hair cascading down her back. Her clear, blue eyes like a china doll's, glistened wide and innocent. But she was not sweet and certainly not innocent.

"Hi, Julia," her friend Carol said, coming around the corner and up the porch steps. "Any more information?"

"I'm getting close," Julia said with irritation.

"What will you do when you have proof?"

"Don't know yet," Julia replied.

"You aren't thinking of doing anything illegal are you?" Carol teased.

"Define illegal," Julia replied.

"Oh, no," Carol said with a little chuckle, "Really, You wouldn't do anything crazy. Would you?"

With a wicked laugh Julia said, "Define crazy."

"Ah, come on, I know you are angry, but really?" Carol mocked.

I made a mistake telling Carol anything, thought Julia. *I should have kept this to myself.* She knew Carol just didn't understand the hours of work she had to put in to find this person, this criminal. Carol didn't understand how those hours of research melted her anger into a ball of soldering lead. Sometimes Julia felt like she would explode from the fury she was feeling. Trying to keep a masked pleasant face was only making it worse.

Especially now because she knew who it was. She knew for certain who was responsible for all the reprehensible acts. But she wasn't telling Carol.

Just then Julia's husband David came out the back door.

Short and a little chunky, he was her partner in crime. His short-sleeved button-down shirt threated to pop at his belly. His thin chicken legs poked through his plaid shorts down to his old black sneakers. Untied of course. His plain face, still pockmarked from adolescent acne, had no redeeming qualities. Teeth a little crooked, hair an unruly, unremarkable brown. But his mind was what drew Julia to him. He understood her. Besides, no other woman gave him a second look. That was a huge plus, since Julia had a nasty jealous streak.

David was guarded as he said a quick hi to Carol.

Then, turning a beaming smile to his wife, he said, "Hey Sweet Cakes, what's up?"

Julia laughed. "I'm just messing with Carol. Spinning tales."

Carol laughed too and said, "You had me going. Well, I gotta go and get dinner. My kids will be circling soon. You are so lucky you don't have to worry about feeding little monsters." She walked back across the driveway to her house.

When David was sure his neighbor was out of hearing range, he went up to Julia. "Oh sugar. What's going on with you? I thought we agreed we would tell no one. Especially not Carol, the town busybody."

Julie gave a long sigh as she brought her slender legs down off the table.

"I was bored. She just goes on and on with all this nonsense stuff about her kids and family. I get tired of hearing it. So I made a mistake. I know it's a mistake. But I took care of it."

She paused then and looked up at him with a mischievous smile and said, "Besides, I found the perp!" With excitement rising in her voice she continued "And he lives right here in town. I found him and he's toast! Aren't you proud of me?"

That news made his body tingle. David leaned down for a deep kiss, "That's my honey."

He felt the anticipation rising up inside him. He knew what was next. God, was he lucky to have found this girl.

A little breathless she said, "So, I think we should do it tonight. I know his wife is out for a book club meeting. I could do it tonight. Are you with me?"

His eyes gleamed down at her. "Oh, baby, you know I am."

They made all the preparations. They had done this before and each time it gave them as much pleasure as the first time. She would make everything right tonight. Justice would prevail. She would show no mercy.

The night was as black as, well, black as night. No moon, no stars, just gathering dark clouds. A thunderstorm on the horizon.

She went up to a little white framed house and knocked on the door. A large man answered.

"Hi," he said as he cleared his throat, "Julia isn't it? The librarian?"

"Yes, that's me. Hi, Mr. Darcy. I wonder is your wife here?"

"No, she's out for a bit. Can I help?"

"Well, it's important library business. Can I wait for her here?" Julia batted her eyelashes at him.

"Oh, sure, ah, yes, I guess, come on in," he answered a little hesitant.

Julia knew his wife Melinda would be out for at least another hour. But she wasn't here for Melinda.

"Would you like something to drink while you wait?" he asked.

"Sure. Do you have lemonade?"

"Oh, yes I do," said Mr. Darcy. "Come sit in here in the kitchen."

Julia felt joy run through her body. *The plan is working just right,* she thought!

As John Darcy got the glasses and ice he was thinking how very happy he was to have this lovely young lady in his kitchen. Even though he was old enough to be her father, he often fantasized about her after coming home from the library. And here she was with her short shorts and tight tank top showing off her lovely young breasts, smiling up at him.

"Do you read much?" Julia asked with childlike interest.

"Well, I guess you know I do. I'm at the library a lot." He laughed as he brought the lemonade to the table.

"Yes, I guess you are. What are you reading now?" she asked.

"I found the new Matty Dalrymple mystery today. And I just finished Todd Harra's <u>Grave Matters</u>. I really enjoy a good mystery."

"Oh, so do I," Julia replied. "Were they good for you?" She said sweetly as she smiled up at him, her innocent eyes wide.

"Yes, ah, yes, in fact they were." Clearly a little rattled, he sat down abruptly across from her, lost in the wondrous depths of her blue eyes.

"Well," she said, "There have been a lot of mysteries missing lately. Have you noticed?"

"Ah. No...ah...I, I didn't," he said, stuttering a little.

Julia lifted her glass and took a little sip. As she moved the glass slowly from her mouth she flicked her tongue over her lips and gave him a slow smile. Her eyes locked on his. Then suddenly her glass tilted and lemonade spilled on her tank top right on her voluminous left breast. "Oh no, look what I've gone and done," she said like a petulant teenager.

"Ah. Oh. Ah, that's okay," his mouth dry as he stared blushing. He then quickly jumped up, stumbling into his chair, and moved across the kitchen to get a towel.

In a swift motion as his back was turned, Julie emptied the powdered contents of a small plastic bag that she had in her hand, right into his drink.

He was so flustered when he moved back to her that at first he tried to wipe the liquid off her top. Realizing what he was doing he just dropped the towel down into her lap.

"Oh, I'm, I'm so sorry,' he stammered. "I just wanted to help."

Her smile was like an angel's as she thanked him profusely taking her time to rub the wet spot in a slow circle while he tried not to stare.

Oh, this is going much better than I thought, she said to herself. She felt intoxicated as she finished and sensuously laid the towel on the table.

"Well here's to good reading." Her voice was like honey as she offered her glass to touch his. "Down the hatch."

She felt a sliver of satisfaction as he drank down half the glass.

Not long now.

"Bottoms up," she said seductively.

The liquid effortlessly went down his throat as she watched with delight.

Suddenly, he began to cough.

"You know," she said with a crooked smile, "You have taken out 17 books and not returned any of them. And you haven't paid any late fines, either."

Watching him weaken she continued with a lilt of malicious pleasure in her voice. "I am making an example of you to all those people who think they can just abuse the library. Taking out books and not returning them is a serious offence. You think there are no consequences, but there are," she finished sharply.

"But, but." he said in between gasps of breath. "I try to return my books but sometimes my wife…in her frenzy to get rid of things..." He coughed and wheezed, "She...she gathers them up too fast and...and sends them off to the Lion's Club." He was losing his strength fast. "She...she volunteers at the library...she just erases the fine." With a limp whisper as he breathed his last breath, "No...no one was supposed to know." He slid to the floor without another word.

The poison worked quickly.

It was over. But Julia realized she had gotten the wrong man...well, *rather* wrong person.

That's all right, she said to herself. I can still fix it. Julie wanted justice even if it took a little longer. She was still aroused. David would be happy.

She made the call.

"Is it done, sweetheart?" he asked breathlessly.

"Yes," she said, "But I have some good news and some bad news."

"Oh, baby," David said with disappointment, "it didn't work?"

"Oh, it did work," she said with a low simmering voice, "and I can't wait to see you. But it was the wrong person. The good news is I know for certain who needs to be punished now. So we just have to do it again, soon."

"We do?" David sighed. "Really? Again? He felt heat pulse through him. "Oh, sugar, hurry home. I'm ready for you."

Her mood was sparkling, and electric, not unlike the lighting flashes in the night sky. It really had become a dark and stormy night with lots of thunder and wildness.

A MAN FROM NANTUCKET

There once was a man from Nantucket

Whose pump failed – with an ice pick she'd stuck it.

She'd snuck up in disguise . . .

But the biggest surprise?

A clean limerick - now you can go suck it.

JANE'S BABY
Chris Bauer

JANE'S BABY answers the question of whatever happened to Jane Roe's baby of Roe v Wade landmark Supreme Court decision fame. Here's a short prologue, then a scene that showcases a hitwoman known as "The Church Hammer."

I want the boy institutionalized, Judge's father told his mother. Try it, his mother said, and I will leave you. His father, a U.S. senator, decided on a different approach: the Marine Corps.

When Judge left for boot camp, they didn't hug, didn't shake hands. There was no imparting of keen insights or wisdom, no fatherly advice. His father made one simple, finally-rid-of-your-bleeping-afflicted-existence comment that came directly from his black heart: *They'll either kill you or cure you.* His father would have been satisfied either way.

Judge's affliction had embarrassed them on the grandest of stages, at President Nixon's second inauguration, when Judge was fourteen. When he turned nineteen, his father wrote the letter. The president said yes, he'd make his enlistment happen. A senator had this access, the Commander-In-Chief this power. That was thirty-eight years ago.

Kill you or cure you.

... Judge waited for his bounty, a bail-jumping pedophile, outside a Shreveport, Louisiana Starbucks. He sat in the van, smooth-talking his K9 deputies, waiting for the guy to exit, wanting, praying the guy would try to run...

Judge had proved his father wrong. The Marines had proved his father wrong. Win-win.

His father died knowing this. His father died horribly. Win-win.

Judge had Tourette Syndrome. There was no cure, but he and his affliction had an arrangement. Win.

His full name, Judge Terrence Drury. His USMC rank at retirement, Gunnery Sergeant. His current profession, bounty hunter. Semper Fi.

~~~

Our hitwoman:

Larinda waited in the church parking lot in an older Ford Explorer SUV, her binoculars raised. Visible through the church's barred windows, Pastor Darlington Beckner flipped through hymnals in a sparsely furnished anteroom behind the altar, smoothing out the rabbit-eared pages, straightening the piles. This was taking longer than she'd expected. Regardless, she would not sully the sanctity of a church.

The pastor hobbled to the door on aged legs and exited the anteroom. Her binoculars followed his progress to the back of the empty church. The Bible passage from the morning service had stayed with her. Matthew 19, verse 14: *"Jesus said, 'Let the little children come to me.'"* His reading was a sign that this was right and just.

One other car was in the lot, the pastor's. He exited the church, pulled the metal door closed behind him, made sure it latched. He paused, lifted his face skyward, breathed in the warm September air.

His wife's recent passing had softened his conservative leanings. This was how The Faithful—capital T, capital F, a religious splinter group—had explained it to Larinda. He'd lost his own gospel, and this made him dangerous. The timing was terrible. A new Texas law now forced women to view ultrasounds of their fetuses before they were allowed to legally terminate their pregnancies. Planned Parenthood appealed the ruling to the Supreme Court. In two weeks the new fall term would begin, and a case from Texas, *Babineau v Turbin,* would be heard. If The Faithful had anything to say about it, the Court would strike down Planned Parenthood's argument, validating the original Texas decision. This validation could be used to overturn *Roe v Wade* in its entirety.

The Faithful began shadowing the pastor thirty years ago. He'd never tried to contact anyone of political, municipal, or jurisprudence consequence, as far as they knew. His marriage back then was dead, but over time it resurrected itself. The Faithful had the reach and the resources to know these things. If he'd felt the urge to confess a certain extramarital transgression to his wife, something they'd used to blackmail him, they were fairly sure he hadn't. Nothing they'd seen had merited any action. Until now.

His first misstep was to contact the FBI. His second was booking a flight to D.C., where they thought he might divulge one consequential miscarriage of duty from his time as the county's adoption agency Director: providing information to The Faithful from records sealed by law, about a certain 1970 closed adoption.

Pastor Beckner was now a new threat to the war on the unborn. A war The Faithful felt was close to being won.

The Faithful. Larinda's confidants and spiritual guides, composed of town elders, captains of industry, televangelists, and politicians. Her clandestine employers on a contract-by-contract basis. They had texted her this morning: *"C.H. Hello. Your new penance is to fix this. The Lord be with you."*

"C.H." Short for *"Church Hammer."*

The pastor unlocked his car. She waited until he climbed inside, so the mess would stay contained.

"Pastor Beckner," she called, approaching his car on foot, dimples accenting her warm smile. "Hello. A moment of your time, please." Her smile widened as she drew closer.

His car window powered the rest of the way down. "Of course, miss. How can I help you?"

Five paces from the car, she raised her right arm, ready to shake his hand. At three paces the small ballistic knife strapped to her wrist inside her jacket ejected from its compressed air sheath with a quiet *thokkk*, the short blade entering his neck, severing his vocal chords. He gripped his throat, a gurgling crimson leak spurting through his fingers onto the steering wheel and dash, asphyxiating him in his own blood. She clapped his shoulder like an old friend and scanned the empty parking lot for inquiring eyes, reconfirming there were no witnesses. She removed the knife from his neck and wiped the blade on his shirt.

"Such a wonderful reading today, Pastor. Thank you, and may you rest in peace."

She reached into his shirt pocket for a jeweled pen, something she'd noticed during his sermon, for proof that she'd carried out the deed. At least she told herself that was the reason for taking it.

Want to read more?

Check out Chris Bauer's recently published novel,

Jane's Baby.

SHE LOUNGED

She lounged at the bar in her seat.

His hand pressed her leg - daring feat!

But when he reached her garter

He found something harder -

This lady - no lady! - packed heat.

THE AMISH AVENGER
Jay Kennedy

I asked myself, not for the first time that night, 'What the hell am I doing here?' But in reality, I knew full well.

The 'here' in that question has a couple of implications. The here-and-now here is the edge of an Amish farmer's field near Oxford PA on a cold snowy night in March. It's a good question. The snow is coming down in Nor'easter proportions – big fat flakes coming down like Stukas over Route 10. But in this case, they would have to be Pennsylvania Dutch dive bombers, not German Junkers. I'm dressed warmly enough.

That's not the point. And that leads to the other implication, the philosophical one. This one is a little clearer to me. No question in my mind that this is exactly what I want to be doing.

But first, a little about me. My name is Robert Scott, universally known as Bobby which is a little weird for a guy in the latter half of his fifties. But Bobby it is, and Bobby it always has been. I lived the passive corporate life for some 30 odd years, and then abruptly dumped my briefcase and frequent flyer miles and took an early retirement.

But watching "Kelly and Ryan" in my pajamas didn't really cut it for me so I decided to follow in the footsteps of my hero Clark Kent and dip my toes into the "Investigative Reporter" racket. Also weird, right? I mean, who just decides to become an "Investigative Reporter" without any prior inclination for journalism? Strike one. While we're at it, why in the world does Oxford need one anyway? It's not like anything ever happens here. There's never even a line at the Post Office during the Christmas season. That pretty much says it all.

Let's be clear. I'm a freelancer which means I don't get paid unless I can uncover and intelligently write stories. Strike two. But surprisingly enough, I'm okay at it.

The story about the big bust of a major Chester County drug dealer who happened to be an Oxfordian? Yep, that was me. The arsonist responsible for burning down both the Octoraro Hotel and the Sunoco station? My byline again. And my current story about the self-proclaimed "Amish Avenger"? It's my biggest one yet.

None of these "Breaking News" exclusives have put me in a favorable light with local Oxford Chief of Police Linda Teel. That hard-driving, no-nonsense flatfoot doesn't like that her small-town police force seems to keep getting upstaged by little ol' me, and can't understand how I keep getting the first, and inside, scoop on what's happening in the underbelly of her town.

But I'm pretty good at being careful and very close lipped about my sources of information, so I've been able to break some big stories before the local coppers had much of an inkling. Judging by how many times they've hauled me in and tried to sweat me for information, I'm guessing that Teel is running out of patience. Tough.

I don't want to give you the idea that Oxford is Camden or anything. It's just a small, sleepy little town that's trying to get it right. Its biggest knock is that it always feels like it's about 45 minutes from civilization. I mean, the closest shopping mall or movie theater is in another state, for crying out loud.

And I defy you to drive through town anytime day or night and not encounter an annoyingly slow Amish horse and buggy that somehow is always in front, never behind, of you. I saw one pull into the drive thru bank line once. You don't see that everyday anywhere else. Laughed right out loud that day.

That leads me back to the "Amish Avenger" story I mentioned. Pennsylvania was once described as "two cities that hate each other divided by the Amish." Clever. Wish I'd thought of that.

The Amish here in PA are different from their brethren in Ohio and Indiana. both of which are bigger than the PA Amish, in terms of number of straw hats running around. One, the PA Amish are much richer. The communities in Ohio and Indiana are poverty level and, secluded as they are, they are all right with that.

But the PA Amish are more entrepreneurial. It seems like there's an Amish Farmers Market or an Amish Furniture Shop on every corner. Think about it, the Amish are supposed to be this peaceful live-amongst-themselves don't-bother-us old world enclave. The plain folk. That's great as long as all that fancy folk non-Amish money keeps flowing into those secluded communities buying quilts, and shoofly pies, and farm fresh vegetables, and the myriad of other Amish products that are hawked everywhere you look.

Two, the PA Amish are much more hypocritical. On the surface, it's all that old-world charm. No modern conveniences, no automation. But I know folks whose only cash paying job is as an Amish Uber, to drive Amish around in their cars to take them from place to place. Can't own an automobile, but willing to pay to ride in one. Anybody see the irony in that?

And God forbid they own a telephone in their home, although it is perfectly okay for them to own and use a phone in their business! They also have no issue with riding their little scooter down the road to a new world neighbor's house so that they can use their newfangled calling device. If no Amish own phones, just who in the hell are they calling anyway?

This so-called "Amish Avenger" storyline I've been writing has really been heating up. Yesterday, this vigilante called Police Dispatch reporting a large Puppy Mill near Oxford. Teel and her squad swept in and rescued hundreds of dogs who were caged and unmercifully neglected. Puppy Mills are a steady stream of income for their operators, both Amish and non-Amish. As long as people continue to buy animals from such dog factories, they continue to pad the owner's pockets with plenty of cold hard cash. I wrote a scathing story about this vile situation, throwing lots of credit Teel's way for emptying this Puppy Mill out.

So now here I sit freezing my ass off on the edge of the field overlooking this empty shell of a building. The Amish Avenger dealt quite a blow to the operation. But all that means is that the owner will get a slap on the wrist, pay some small fine, and will soon be back in business.

Not if I can help it, I think, and my bones creak and crack as I stand from where I've been hunkered down. The gasoline from the can I'm carrying sloshes over my heavy boots as I make my way through the field towards the building. No electricity here so no lights showing but the bright Pennsylvania moon in the cloudless Chester County sky provides plenty of illumination for me as I splash my accelerant around the wooden barn.

Tomorrow's story detailing the terrible fire that destroyed the insidious and just vacated Puppy Mill has already been written. The Amish Avenger strikes again. My match flares and I toss it toward the barn. The whoosh of the flame warms both my body and my soul. As I walk away back across the field, I mutter "Adopt, don't shop."

Damn straight.

BOY AIN'T RIGHT

Scott Pruden

Miranda leaned against the kitchen doorway drying her hands with a dishcloth. "Randy, when you gonna finally take Bobby hunting?"

Randy was acutely focused on the race from Talladega, but he heard her perfectly. "Because, Miranda, your brother is a retard, and he's got no business being out in the woods with squirt gun, let alone a shotgun."

He swirled his can of Coors Light to assess how much was left. Not much. He was thirsty for a fourth, but Miranda was blocking his path to the kitchen of the narrow singlewide. If he'd had a few more he'd just smack her out of the way, but he was still feeling mellow. He could see that ending soon.

"What'd I tell you about calling him that? Only people who use that word anymore are school kids, anyway. I wish you'd get it through your head that he has Down syndrome and stop treating him so bad."

Randy stared at the monolithic big-screen he'd nearly sold his soul for about fifteen years before. Enough overtime at the plant and he'd be able to replace it with one of those sweet flat screens soon and sell this massive piece of crap over at the swap meet. Of course, that was assuming he didn't beat the hell out of his wimpy little college boy supervisor first.

Randy looked at his girlfriend with tired eyes. "Miranda, honey, he don't know the difference." He turned back to the race and took another long swig.

Her hands went to her hips. "That's so unfair and so mean. Of course he knows the difference!"

He'd gotten her back up now. Pretty soon he figured he'd have to beat it back down. This uppity shit got old fast.

"You want proof? What does Bobby do at the mall?"

"He's on the security detail."

"Yeah, but what's he *really* do?"

"Well, he patrols the food court and helps sweep up and wipe the tables."

"And how'd you describe all the other people who do that?"

"I … um …"

"How about *RE*-TARDS, Miranda?"

She turned away. He could hear her sniffing quietly.

The race progressed and he turned up the volume, filling the tiny living room with the roar of supercharged American stock engines.

Dale Jr. blew a tire about two laps later and pulled into the pit under a yellow flag. In about three more laps the front door opened.

"Home!" Bobby announced, a little too loud like always. He stood on the tiny entry porch and brushed the cuffs of his black cargo pants. It had been a dry fall, and they were dusted with red clay from walking the half-mile from the bus stop at the entrance of the trailer court.

Miranda turned, wiped her eyes and forced a smile. "Hey, sweetie. You have a good day?"

"Hey, Sissy." He had come in and was concentrating on removing his belt – his utility belt, he called it – when Randy grunted a hello.

Bobby ignored him as he took off his blue uniform shirt that bore his name over the left breast pocket, just like Randy's work shirt, to reveal – *what the hell?* – a Batman t-shirt. Randy remembered him saying something about being part of building security meaning he was a real crime fighter, but this shit was ridiculous.

"Going to feed Cashew," Bobby said, breaking free of his sister's tight hug and moving quickly to the back yard.

"Cashew?" Randy muttered.

"Remember that squirrel that the neighbor boy shot with his BB gun? Bobby found him in the yard the other day and he's been nursing him back to health in the rabbit hutch out back. I was pretty sure that little thing was as good as dead, but as soon as Bobby called to him, he came limping right on up. That boy just seems to have a way. I'd swear sometimes that little thing knows just what he's saying. It's pretty amazing."

Randy sniffed. "Sure, amazing. Amazing that kid is such a shitty shot. When I shoot something, it stays dead." He drained the last of his beer.

"So, hunting tomorrow?"

Jesus, she just wouldn't let it drop.

"You don't even have to give him a gun. You know how he is about animals. He wouldn't want to shoot anything. I just want the two of you to spend some time together. I'm working tonight, so can I trust you to do this one thing for me?"

Randy crumpled the can into a deformed hourglass.

"Fine. We'll go out early. I've got an extra vest he can use so he don't get himself shot."

Even though he couldn't imagine why the world would miss another useless retard.

#

At eleven-thirty that night, Miranda, still wearing her scrubs from the nursing home, pushed Bobby's bedroom door open a crack to check on him before she took her post-shift shower.

"Hey, Sissy," Bobby murmured from the bed.

"Hey, sweetie," she said as she sat on the edge of the twin. "You're still up. You OK?"

"Yeah. Just thinking."

"What about?" She reached down to stroke the cowlick at his hairline. He was quiet for a moment, but his brow was furrowed like he was trying to figure something out.

"Sissy, when Randy hits you, that's wrong, ain't it?"

Miranda gasped and covered her mouth. "Oh, sweetie, I'm so sorry …" She tried to hold back the tears, but some escaped anyway. Then after a moment, she calmed down, wiped her eyes and said, "It's a grown-up thing, OK? I don't want you to worry about me."

"But if it's wrong, that makes him a criminal, right?"

"Well, sweetie … see, it's more complicated than that."

"No, it's not. He hurts you. He hurts you a lot and he lies. He lies about everything, and I know he lies to you all the time. So he's a bad guy. And I'm a crime fighter like Batman, so I should do something about it, right?"

She looked behind her to make sure Randy wasn't lurking in the doorway. The noise from the TV – now some blowhard on the news going off about taking the country back from the Mexicans, blacks and Muslims – blared from the living room, but that didn't mean he was still there.

"Honey, you need to hush, OK?" She gazed into his eyes, then cupped her hand to his cheek. There was stubble there. Mentally, he would be a boy forever, but at seventeen, physically and chronologically he was a man. Ever since that trucker, drunk on lack of sleep and operating in a crystal meth haze, had crushed their parents' minivan like a soda can, it had been her job to try to help him become a good man in a world convinced he was inferior. Sometimes she wished their parents were still around to do that instead. Maybe things would be different.

"Randy's just got a bad temper, is all. And don't you think you're supposed to do anything, babe. I'm a big girl and I can take care of myself."

"If you could take care of yourself he'd be in jail, I think."

Miranda was quiet.

"Just don't you let this Batman stuff go to your head and get you hurt. I don't need you coming to my rescue. If we can keep from making him too upset, we don't have anything to worry about, right?"

Bobby was quiet for a minute. "If you say so. But even if he doesn't get caught hurting you, I bet he's still going to mess up somehow."

"Just you hush. I don't want to hear any more about it." Miranda kissed him on the forehead, and he rolled over and went to sleep.

#

It was going to be one of those weird November Indian summer days, so Randy didn't want to layer up too much in case it really did get as hot as the weatherman was saying. Bobby was already up and dressed, sitting on his bed eating Cap'n Crunch out of the box while he watched some old Bugs Bunny cartoon on TV. Elmer Fudd was getting the shit end of the deal again.

Randy stood in the door and took it all in. Damn Batman was everywhere, plastered from floor to ceiling with more stuff than he'd ever seen outside of a comic book store. The whole room was a gallery of the glowering, cowled vigilante. Randy never could understand the appeal. Freak in tights and a mask, like some pervy fag from a damn S&M club.

"If you're coming with you me you better get your ass in gear, Bobby."

"Right there!"

"And please hush. The last thing I need is your loud ass waking up your sister. Lord knows she's a bitch on wheels if she gets woken up after a late shift."

"Gotta feed Cashew."

Jesus. The damn squirrel.

"Well, make it quick."

Randy took his Winchester and a box of shells from the hall closet, then followed Bobby out the back door. The kid was holding a red Solo cup half filled with shelled pecans as he opened the door to the rabbit hutch. The shot-up squirrel, his left shoulder wrapped in gauze bandage, perked right up and ran into Bobby's hand.

"Hey, Cashew," he said real soft and somehow not sounding quite so much like a retard. "How're you feeling, little guy?"

The squirrel looked at Bobby and cocked its head sideways just like Randy's old bird dog, Buelah, would when she was confused. Then it chittered what seemed just like an answer to the question.

"That's good! You eat these up and I'll get you some more when I get home, OK?"

Randy sighed and tapped his foot. "Bobby, we doing this or not?"

Then damn if Bobby and the little piece of shit squirrel didn't both turn and look at him like they were two old ladies and he'd just farted in church. The yard rat chittered something else.

"Going hunting. Don't you worry. I'll be fine. More nuts when I get home, OK?"

That seemed to be it. Off Bobby's hand he hopped, and he was back in the hutch like it was his own little bachelor apartment.

Bobby turned and leveled a gaze at him. "You got your hunting license?"

What the hell? "Yeah … what's it matter to you?"

"Gun permit?"

"Got that, too. What's your problem, anyway?"

Bobby looked him dead in the eye, then in his annoying, mush-mouth way, said "Just trying to make sure you're not doing anything *illegal*. OK, let's go."

He was off to the passenger side of the truck before Randy even had a chance to tell him to hurry the hell up.

"Your plate's about to expire, too. And your inspection's due next month."

Jesus. Suddenly the kid's the world's most annoying retard cop.

"And don't forget your seatbelt," Bobby said as he buckled his.

Randy slid into the driver's seat and ignored him.

The ride out to Lester DuBose's farm was about fifteen minutes, and Randy's goal was to take up as many of those minutes as possible with the radio turned up too loud to do much talking. Of course that didn't make a bit of difference to Bobby.

"Speed limit here is 45. You're going 62."

"You planning to drive, Bobby?" There was no answer from the passenger seat, just Bobby staring straight ahead, then sniffing and wiping his nose on the sleeve of his hoodie like he hadn't said a word.

Didn't think so, dumbass.

And just to prove a point, Randy gunned the engine to push the speedometer needle well past 70.

"Too bad I'm not driving," Bobby said out of nowhere.

"Oh yeah? Why's that?" Randy had never heard the kid this uppity. So far he'd never laid a hand on him. That might have to change.

"'Cause I'd have seen that speed trap you just passed."

Sure enough, Randy checked the mirror and saw blue and red lights emerge from a break in the trees behind him.

"Shit, Bobby, why didn't you say something?" Randy hissed as he pulled to the shoulder. Bobby just sat there, and Randy was pretty sure he saw the kid crack a little smile.

"Nothin' to worry about," Randy said, trying to reassure himself. "I got an in with the folks at the sheriff's department. This won't take but a sec. Bobby, how 'bout you reach in the glove box and grab me my registration and insurance card."

"Please?"

What the hell? Who did this kid think he was all of a sudden?

"I swear to god, I'm gonna ..."

"Do what? There's a policeman right there."

Randy stared dead into Bobby's beady eyes. His teeth clenched, he growled, "*Please.*"

"Morning," said a female voice. Randy turned to the window and wondered if the look on his face betrayed his disappointment. Instead of one of his sheriff's deputy drinking buddies, it was some butch-ass lady state trooper. "License and registration, please."

While Bobby fished the documents from the glove box, she unholstered her flashlight and scanned the inside of the cab. The beam lingered over the shotgun mounted behind them.

"Where you off to so fast this morning?"

"Doing a little hunting, ma'am. Got my girlfriend's brother with me today." Randy hoped that would garner some sympathy, but he wasn't counting on it.

She looked over his documentation, then held them up. "I'll be back with these in a moment."

Like an asshole, Randy said, "Thank you, ma'am."

Bobby actually snickered. "I like your manners a lot better when you're talking to lady police officers."

Randy sat and seethed, white-knuckling the steering wheel with both hands while he watched her return to her cruiser. Both of them sat in silence until the trooper returned.

"Mr. McDade, do you know why I stopped you this morning?"

"Um, speeding, I guess."

"That's correct. I clocked you going 78 in a zone clearly posted 45 miles an hour. I'm going to issue you a citation for going 30 miles over the posted limit. And I'm sure you're aware that state law requires all drivers to wear a seatbelt. I notice you're not wearing yours this morning, so I'm adding that to the fine, as well," she said as she ripped the ticket from her pad. "And please remember to keep the safety of others in mind. I'm going to do you a favor by not asking to see the permit for that weapon, but I'd hate to respond to another incident where you're behaving in an unsafe fashion."

"Unsafe for him or for someone else?" Bobby piped up.

The trooper shined the beam on Bobby's face. "Either."

Randy heard Bobby snicker again. "Yes, ma'am," he said.

#

After the trooper drove off, Randy cussed under his breath as he buckled his seatbelt, then turned the radio up loud and accelerated again, this time keeping the speedometer pegged at the posted limit.

"How much longer?"

"Seriously, Bobby, you're about to get on my last nerve. Just keep your hole shut, OK?"

"Or what?"

"Or I'm gonna … Nevermind. I'm in enough trouble already."

After about five more miles, Randy pulled onto the shoulder and made the turn onto the narrow dirt road that led onto Lester DuBose's property. He had free access to the wooded side of

Lester's land just as long as he stayed close to the highway side and away from Lester's cows. Even though he let Miranda do all the housework at home, in the interest of maintaining his deal with Lester, Randy always made sure to clean up his empties.

They pulled up to the twin iron swing gates and Randy turned the volume down.

"All right, Bobby, here's the deal. I'm just doing this as a favor to your sister, so don't think this makes us best buds or nothin'. I brought you an orange vest and you got to wear it so you won't get shot, 'cause Lord knows I'd never hear the end of that. But you got to understand – stay behind me and hush. If you see me raise this shotgun, you stop whatever you're doing, shut up and freeze. We clear?"

"Yep."

"Good. Last thing I need is to have to explain to your sister why I'm bringing you home full of buckshot. And if possible, I'd like to have some chance of actually shooting something."

Randy pulled the truck to a stop and climbed out to swing the right gate open. Looking back to the truck cab against the glare of the headlights, he saw Bobby's stupid face. It was lit up by the truck's dome light, the kid looking back at him with the same mouth-breather expression he always had. Damn if he didn't find himself thinking how nice it would be if he'd never have to worry about bringing him home again.

The light wouldn't be breaking over the trees for another hour or so, giving Randy ample time to get out to the deer stand along the narrow, dusty path that passed as a road.

"You ain't afraid of heights, are you?"

"No. Why? Where we going?"

Randy wheeled the truck off the dirt road and stopped. Glinting in the headlight beam was an aluminum extension ladder going up the side of a tree and stopping at a tiny platform about twenty feet above the ground.

"Awesome! Is that a tree house?"

"No, you ... No. It's a deer stand. We'll wait up there until we spot something, and that way we ... *I* can get a clean shot on a deer without scaring it off."

"I don't know. A treehouse sounds like a lot more fun. I don't like killing things, anyway."

"It's called 'hunting,' Bobby, not 'watching.' What'd you think I was coming out here to do, anyway, play with myself?"

"I know who you like to come out here and play with." He fixed Randy with a penetrating gaze.

Randy got the odd sensation that somehow the kid had gotten a peek inside his head. He tried not to look guilty about it. "Oh, yeah? Who's that?"

"Never mind. Let's get on up there so you can shoot something and hope it stays dead."

Bobby opened the door and hopped out.

"Hey! What the hell is that supposed to mean?"

Randy turned the truck off, pulled the shotgun down from the back window rack and scrambled to catch up, but Bobby had already slipped on the orange safety vest and was halfway up the ladder.

"No beer this morning?"

Randy paused in mid ascent and looked up to the tiny platform, where Bobby was peering over the edge.

"What? What the hell kind of question is that?"

"Just wondering."

Kid sees more than I thought. Got to be more discrete.

The first hour passed quietly, with nothing more than the sounds of the forest and the occasional growl of a logging truck downshifting on the highway to break the silence. Randy kept his eye on the salt lick he'd hung on a big loblolly pine about twenty yards from the stand, hoping something would show up for a treat, but so far no luck.

"Randy, I'm getting hungry. Can I have a snack?"

"Yeah, but make it quiet."

That was apparently the kid's cue to make as much noise as humanly possible, taking what seemed like five solid minutes to get the foil wrapper off a store-bought granola bar.

"Jesus Christ, Bobby," Randy hissed. "You trying to scare away every damn thing in these woods?"

"Sorry. I'm done."

He crammed the wrapper into his hoodie pocket, but then made enough noise with his chewing that Randy's teeth ground. He glared at Bobby, hoping he'd get the hint, but was distracted by rustling below.

And there, its massive head bent low over the salt lick, was a buck the likes of which he'd only seen in his dreams or those cable TV hunting shows. And the rack – holy Hell... He counted twelve points just from eyeballing him from this distance. The wind changed direction for a split second and the buck looked up to check for a scent on the breeze.

Randy glared at Bobby, watching the boy's eyes get big as his jaw stopped moving. He turned his attention back to the buck and shouldered the shotgun, sighting down the barrel and gently laying a finger over the trigger guard as he drew a bead on the huge beast's neck.

He held steady and moved his finger off the guard and onto the trigger itself. *Just a little pressure, and I'll have the kill of a lifetime.*

The *deedle-dee* ringtone of his phone seemed to echo through the woods for an eternity before he could fumble into his vest pocket, fish it out and read the name "Roxy" on the screen. *What the hell was she doing calling now?*

"Hey," he whispered into the phone. "No, I'm out at DuBose's place. No, you can't come. I'm here with Miranda's brother. What? No, no way. Listen, I've got a one in a million shot here that you probably just made me miss, so can I just call you back later? Fine. You, too."

"Who was that?" Bobby whispered too loud.

"A friend of mine. Don't you worry about it."

"Your phone said it was Roxy. Isn't there a Roxy that works down at the Racetrack Grill? I've talked to her before. She's pretty. But I don't think she likes Sissy too much."

Randy was ready to tell him to hush, but was curious about what he'd say next. "Really? Why's that?"

"She's always real nice to me, but every time she talks to Sissy she looks like she smells dog poop."

Sounds about right, Randy thought.

"So why'd she want to meet you?"

"Don't you worry about that. It don't matter anyway. She sure as hell blew that …"

Randy looked down at the salt lick and had to blink a couple of times before he believed what he saw. The buck was still there, looking up at him like it was waiting to hear the rest of his story.

"Holy … Bobby, be real quiet for me, OK?"

He aimed again, this time determined not to hesitate. Randy got the deer's front flank in his sights and eased over to fall again on the neck.

He pulled the trigger and the recoil pounded his shoulder, the thunderous report echoing through the trees.

The buck dropped where it had stood. "C'mon, Bobby. Let's go check him out."

Bobby uncovered his ears. "Is he dead?"

"If he ain't then I don't know what's gonna kill him. That shot was perfect."

They scrambled down the ladder and both ran up to the deer. Randy heard the beast huff through its nostrils, but it was circling the drain fast. It bleated as he grabbed its rack and lifted, marveling at its heft.

"That's a thing of beauty, ain't it?"

Bobby just stood there for a minute, looking like he was thinking something over real hard. Then he kneeled beside the deer, leaning over his ear like he was whispering something.

"Whatcha doin', Bobby? You're gonna need to move out of the way, 'cause if this big boy don't die soon I'm gonna have to take other measures."

Randy unsheathed his field knife, ready to slit the buck's jugular and be done with it, but Bobby didn't move. He just knelt there, whispering something to the dying deer and stroking its bloodied neck.

"Bobby? Seriously, you got to move."

Nothing. Just more whispering.

"Bobby! Damn it, can you not be such a god damn retard for one second?"

The buck bleated again, then jerked its head and freed its rack from Randy's hands.

"What the…"

It jerked a second time and Randy was silent, unsure of what he felt. Then he looked down and saw it – an antler, its tip sharpened against a forest full of pine bark, had sunk into his chest, his life pouring out around it like someone had opened a Coke can that had been shaken up.

Before all went black, the last thing he saw was Bobby standing and brushing himself off. The kid leveled his gaze, any shred of sympathy absent.

"So much for you shooting something and it staying dead, I guess."

#

Bobby gingerly lifted the phone out of Randy's pocket and turned to watch the deer ease itself back onto its feet as the buckshot pellets emerged from its flesh like they were being pulled by a magnet. The beast wobbled, shaking Randy's dead weight off his rack, then gained its footing and ambled toward him, nuzzling the boy's head with his snout. Bobby knew from what Cashew had told him it would take a few days for the wounds to heal completely and that the deer would be sore for a while.

"I'm sorry he shot you, but you won't have to worry about him anymore, OK? Just don't go back to those salt licks. That's asking for trouble."

The beast huffed, nuzzled Bobby once more and limped back into the pines, the tips of its antlers still moist with Randy's blood, a crimson shred of his flannel shirt dangling off one point like the safety flags that hung off the back of the logging trucks.

Bobby climbed into the cab of the pickup and dialed 911, telling the dispatcher only that there had been a hunting accident and he was worried that his sister's boyfriend might be dead.

The ambulance arrived just after the lady trooper who'd stopped them earlier, and the nice EMTs helped him clean off some of the blood that had transferred when he was bent over the buck. The trooper was real nice, too, and asked him some questions about what happened. Bobby told her and didn't even have to lie. He just left out a few details. After that the lady from family services came to get him and drove him home to Sissy, who met him at the door in her PJs and cried and hugged him tight and asked him if he was OK.

"I'm sorry, Sissy."

"For what, sweetie?"

"You worked late last night. I really didn't want to wake you up."

#

Miranda stood at the back screen door, bleary from crying and not enough sleep. She held her phone in her hand, having just hung up with Roxy, the waitress from the Racetrack Grill who always seemed to give Randy a little too much attention.

"We're really going to miss him," the woman had said through her own tears. "Let me know if there's anything I can do."

Here's what you can do. How about go to Hell, Miranda thought, wondering just how long she'd been oblivious to what Randy was up to. Figures that the woman he'd chosen to cheat with was as dumb as a box of rocks. She'd called on Randy's phone, her name and cheesy glamour photo appearing as a favorite contact like it was nothing. A minute of poking around and Miranda found a dirty book's worth of naked pictures and filthy texts between the two going back eight months. *Son of a bitch.*

Then she remembered what Bobby had said about Randy, and how he knew that Randy was lying to her all the time.

Bobby was behind her with his red cup full of pecans. "'Scuse me, Sissy. Got to go feed Cashew."

She gave him room to exit then poured another cup of coffee. From the open window over the sink she could observe him less obviously, and marveled again at the care he'd given the wounded squirrel. Just like she would with one of her nursing home residents, he delicately checked under the squirrel's bandage.

"Looks like your shoulder's all better, Cashew."

Cashew chattered and seemed to test the injured joint, then climbed up into Bobby's hand and chattered again while pointing to her brother.

Miranda leaned forward, unsure of what she was witnessing.

Bobby looked down at his Batman t-shirt, which he would wear under his work uniform with his name on the patch over the left breast pocket. "That? That's the Batman symbol. He's a famous crimefighter. That means he stops bad people and sends them to jail."

Cashew made a squeak and a chitter.

"No, he's not real. He's from comics and the movies."

More squeaks from Cashew.

"Me, a crimefighter?"

Another long string of chatter.

"You really think so? Well, thanks, I guess. I just had to do something to make sure Sissy was OK and he couldn't hurt her. If he was in jail he might be able to get out. Now he won't bother us no more."

The coffee cup dropped from her hand and shattered in the sink, and she had to brace herself against the counter's edge to keep from collapsing while she tried to process what she was hearing. Going over in her mind every terrible thing her brother must have seen and heard between her and Randy – his drunken rages, the screaming, the bruises and black eyes, the sound of her pleading to stay when he threatened to kick them out – she understood now all that he had told her the night before.

As Miranda watched, Randy put his palm up to the formerly wounded squirrel, who in return raised its tiny paw and gave Bobby what to Miranda's eyes looked like just like a high-five.

"So, that's it, buddy. I guess you're all set to go."

Bobby stood aside, and the squirrel vaulted from the hutch and made its way to the chain link fence along the back yard, scampering up and over, then disappearing into the pines.

A slam of the screen door and Bobby was there next to her, looking at the shards of her coffee mug. "You OK, Sissy?"

Miranda enveloped him, pulling his head close in to her shoulder and sobbing hard, letting out the shame and rage and disappointment she'd been holding onto for so very long. He held her in return, saying nothing as she wept like she didn't know how to stop.

But eventually she did, and after she'd wiped her nose and dried her eyes on a square of paper towel, she held Bobby at arm's length.

"You know, honey, you're the man of the house now, so that means you're in charge of taking care of us, right?"

Bobby looked back, and a glimmer of fully developed adult determination shone through whatever delays or defects people said he had. He pulled her close again.

"Don't worry, Sissy," he said. "I already was."

THE EIGHTH CIRCLE
Sarah Cain

"We're all dying, so we might as well get on with it."

Danny Ryan looked at the words scrawled across his laptop with some satisfaction and winced. He almost felt his grandmother's boney knuckle rap against the back of his head.

"Blasphemer. Do y'think He died on the cross for you to dismiss life so lightly?"

"I'm not dismissing life. I'm saying we're all headed to one end," Danny said aloud. Then he realized how ridiculous it was to argue with a dead woman.

"'I spit in the face of Time.'"

"Yeats again? Really?" But she was gone, and he was losing his mind by inches. He slammed the laptop shut.

Danny wanted to hurl the goddamn machine across the room. What happened to the words that used to flow out of his brain, through his fingers, onto the keyboard? What good was a columnist who couldn't write?

But he wasn't a columnist anymore. He was, what? His mind skittered through the possibilities: dumbass, delinquent, decayed. So many D words, but not the one he wanted.

Leaning back in his leather chair, he picked up the photograph of his son that sat on his desk to the left of the laptop. Conor wore his purple soccer jersey and sported a bruise on his forehead. His huge grin showcased his missing right front tooth, and he clutched his MVP trophy in his small hands like it was the World Cup.

Danny set the photograph back on the desk and forced back the surge that threatened to drown him. He opened his drawer and pulled out an old Tokarev TT-33, and then stood and walked to the stone hearth. When he sat next to Beowulf, the dog laid his massive head across Danny's knees. He stroked Beowulf's black fur. Beowulf licked his face.

"This was my grandfather's" Danny held up the gun and drew a bead on the computer. He then turned the gun around and pointed it at his temple. "The old man gave it to me, Wolf. You know why?" He pulled the trigger. The gun clicked, and Danny set it on the hearth. "He said it was the perfect gun for a Commie asshole."

Outside, the sound of splintering wood brought Danny to his feet. Beowulf tore into the kitchen and hurled himself at the door, barking loud enough to raise the dead. Danny left the gun on the hearth and followed. He grabbed his parka, cell phone, and a flashlight, and pushed Beowulf back from the door. "Wolf, you stay here."

Following the beam of the light through the wind-driven sleet, he saw the hole in the fence. A car balanced precariously on the small island of ornamental shrubbery in the middle of the duck pond. Whoever sat in the car wasn't trying to get out.

Rain stung Danny's face. The wind slapped his skin, and tiny pellets of ice beat against him. He called 9-1-1 and then clambered down the slippery incline.

The flashlight lit up the back of the car, and Danny froze. Jesus.. He knew that old black BMW with its "Ahh, I See the Screw-Up Fairy Has Visited Us Again" bumper sticker.

Michael Cohen. They'd fought. It seemed long ago now. The wet seeped under Danny's coat, and he shoved his phone into his pocket. He heard a crunch, and the front end of the BMW dipped into the water.

Danny sloshed into the pond. It wasn't that deep, but the freezing water sent shock waves up his legs. He stumbled in the sucking mud, and the flashlight slid from his wet hand. For a moment, it illuminated the pond in eerie green and then blinked out. He grabbed the door handle with numb fingers and wrenched it open.

In the glow of the overhead light, he could see the smashed windshield and Michael draped over the steering wheel. No airbags in this heap. Danny pushed Michael back as gently as he could, careful to avoid the shattered glass. Blood bubbled from Michael's nose and mouth and oozed down the front of his blue jacket. Michael gave a shuddering wheeze, and his eyes blinked open. His round face looked slack.

Danny could hear the faint call of sirens now. "Don't try to talk. Help's coming." The metallic stench of blood assaulted him. "It'll be all right, Michael."

Michael shuddered. "Danny." Rasping coughs shook his husky frame, and flecks of bloody foam hit Danny in the face. "I . . . I love you. Y'know? Brothers."

Danny knew Michael didn't have much time. He leaned closer. "What happened?"

"So sorry," Michael's voice came slow and thick. The light in his eyes faded with each word.

"Sorry? Sorry for what? Michael?" Police cars and an ambulance screeched around the curve. Red-and-blue lights reflected off the black water. Michael's head drooped down. When he gave a rattling wheeze, Danny grasped his shoulders. "Michael?"

Michael lifted his head enough that his lips brushed Danny's ear. "Inferno."

To read what happens next,

get Sarah Cain's first novel, *The Eighth Circle.*

OUR DANCING DAYS
Matty Dalrymple

A hall, a hall, give room!—And foot it, girls.—
More light, you knaves! And turn the tables up,
And quench the fire. The room is grown too hot.—
Ah, sirrah, this unlooked-for sport comes well.—
Nay, sit, nay, sit, good cousin Capulet,
For you and I are past our dancing days.

William Shakespeare
Romeo & Juliet

ANN KINNEAR SAT in the empty dance studio, listening to "Cuando Me Enamoro" start up on the CD player. Over the antiseptic smell of heavy-duty cleaner, she could pick up the faint scent of garlic from the pizza shop downstairs.

It was her fifth evening in the studio, but the first alone. The first four had been spent with her client, the widow of one of the seven people who had died here less than a month before.

The studio still bore the marks of the attack. Only fragments of the room-length mirror clung to a bullet-riddled wall. The shards that had littered the floor and created a razor-sharp bed for the people who had fallen had been cleared away once the yellow crime scene tape had been taken down. The wooden floor had been scrubbed, but dark stains remained where the victims had lain. The small refrigerator that once held bottles of water for the dancers stood quiet, its cord unplugged, its door propped open. Only the artificial ferns that decorated each corner of the room appeared untouched by the attack.

The casualties among the dance class students had been five instead of six because Ann's client, Miranda Gorman, had been home with a migraine that night.

"Alan went to class because he had to return a putter he had borrowed from Travis," Miranda explained when she booked the engagement with Ann's brother and business manager, Mike. "Plus, he figured he could get in a couple of turns with Trina—she's the main instructor—and then teach me when he got home, so we wouldn't be so far behind. Our daughter's wedding was at the end of the month, and we didn't want to embarrass ourselves on the dance floor." Her voice cracked on the last word.

The casualties among the instructors had been one instead of two because Trina had been spared. Ann had seen two photos of Trina Hochmann in the online coverage of the attack. In one, she spun, graceful and smiling, across a dance floor in the arms of a handsome, dark-haired man, her gown belling out around her. In the other, two EMTs flanked her, supporting her into the back of an ambulance after the attack. The blood on her hands and clothes had proven not to be hers, but the blasted look in her eyes showed she had not escaped unscathed.

Trina had left town after the attack to escape the media frenzy, and had made it clear that she had no intention of returning to the studio she had founded with her previous partner—the handsome man in the dance competition photo, and the perpetrator of the attack—four years before.

Miranda and Alan Gorman's daughter's wedding had been postponed. Not only was the father of the bride dead, and the mother of the bride barely functional, but six of victims had been on the guest list.

The owner of the pizza shop downstairs owned the building. Not surprisingly, no business had yet expressed interest in setting up shop at the scene of the Dance Hall Massacre, as the more sensational news outlets had labeled it, and he had been willing to give Miranda a key for her evening visits to the studio with Ann. Miranda told Ann that he had also proven to be effective at clearing the building's parking lot of news vans and paparazzi.

"How does he do that?" asked Ann.

"He's … imposing-looking," said Miranda.

It was Miranda who insisted that they play Latin music. "Alan *loved* the rumba," she said. "He would have been happy if that's the only dance we ever did." She blotted her raw, red-rimmed nose. "He was good at it, too."

So for four evenings, Ann and Miranda had arrived at the studio at eight o'clock—the time when the weekly dance class had begun—and, sitting on the folding metal chairs that lined one wall, listened to one Latin song after the other. Miranda glanced at her watch at least once a minute, and at eight fifty-three each night, she would give a little hitching breath and drop her head onto her clenched hands.

"Ten minutes later," she said. "Ten minutes later and he would have been gone, on his way home."

"You don't need to be here," Ann said gently. "You could wait outside, and if he shows up, I could call you."

"No, I have to be here," said Miranda. "What if he only shows up for a minute? I might miss him." She twisted the tissue in her fingers. "I was hoping he would have a message for Caitlin."

"I don't think it's always possible for them to communicate. Sometimes they don't … hang around."

"He was so excited about the wedding," said Miranda, seeming not to have heard Ann. "Walking Caity down the aisle, the father-daughter dance …" She blew her nose. "They were going to dance to 'My Girl' by The Temptations."

"Rumba?"

Miranda shot Ann a look and, evidently deciding Ann's question was sincere, nodded.

"Yes. I saw them practice once—they looked so …"

She kneaded the sodden ball of her tissue.

Then, each night at nine o'clock, Miranda snapped her purse closed and stood up. "Looks like it won't be tonight."

"I could stay a while longer," said Ann the first night.

Miranda shook her head. "No, we always left class on the dot of nine. I think he'll come between eight and nine. Same time tomorrow?"

The dance studio was in Gaithersburg, Maryland—almost three hours from West Chester, Pennsylvania, by back roads, a theoretical two-and-a-quarter by 95, but that route cut right through Baltimore and was no doubt liable to delays. It seemed too long for a daily commute to and from West Chester, where Ann had grown up and where her brother Mike still lived, and too short to ask Ann's occasional charter pilot, Walt, to come down from the Adirondacks to fly her back and forth. She could have hired a pilot in West Chester, but it seemed an unnecessary extravagance to ask Miranda to foot that bill.

Miranda was, however, happy to pay for lodgings at the Gaithersburg Courtyard, so Ann was finding ways of killing the twenty-three hours a day she wasn't spending in the dance studio with Miranda. One day she drove into Washington and, unable to find a parking space, drove back to Gaithersburg. Another day she drove to Seneca Creek State Park and took the unofficial *Blair Witch Project* self-guided tour. She saw no spirits. The other days she spent most of the time in her hotel room, binge reading Stephen King.

On the fifth night, Miranda was stricken by a migraine again, and Ann went to the studio alone. She dutifully inserted a CD into the venerable multi-CD player—she was relieved to find a box of CDs helpfully labeled "Rumba"—and wandered aimlessly around the room. There wasn't much to see. She entered the small office and stepped to a bulletin board with a patchwork of papers thumbtacked to it, including a printout of an online article from a site called *The Town Courier*. It was another photo of Trina dancing, her smile not the false accessory of a well-trained performer, but a genuine expression of joy, her eyes locked on her partner's. This one was a different partner than in the photo the media had used—a younger man with unruly red hair who returned her joyful expression.

Ann read the caption: *Our own Dancing Star, Trina Hochmann, competing at the Mid-Atlantic Ballroom Competition finals with new partner, Travis Burch.*

Ann glanced through the other items on the board—another article about Trina and Travis, this one from an actual print newspaper, a list of class fees, a diagram of pre-dance stretching exercises—then wandered back into the studio.

She glanced at her phone: eight twenty-three. If she followed Miranda's schedule, thirty-seven minutes to go.

She resumed her seat on one of the folding chairs. After a minute, she glanced at her phone again, then, a bit guiltily, opened the ereader app: *The Stand*. She couldn't imagine that her reading would keep Alan from appearing if he wanted to. And she was at an exciting part.

.Some time later, deep into King's description of the ravages of Captain Trips, she became aware of a light tapping noise. She glanced at the time: nine-oh-three. The time of the attack, eight-fifty-three, had come and gone unnoticed.

She put her phone aside, but the tapping had stopped. She resumed reading, but a minute later became aware of the tapping once again. She crossed to the CD player and turned the volume down on Santana's 'Primavera.'

After a moment, she heard it again. It seemed to be coming from the stairway that led to the front door.

She went to the top of the stairs and looked down. All she could see through the glass front door was a small square of concrete walkway.

"Miranda?" she called.

There was no answer.

Ann descended the steps slowly. When she reached the bottom, she peered out of the locked door. The light in the entryway cast onto the walkway a backwards shadow of the script on the glass: "Sentimental Journey Dance Studio."

"Miranda?" she called again.

Still no answer.

She flipped the lock and stepped outside. There wasn't a soul in sight, and nowhere a prankster could be hiding. Mike's Audi, which Ann had borrowed for the trip, was the only car parked in front of the pizza shop. Maybe she would call it a night and stop by for a slice.

"I'm glad you're—" she heard from not more than a couple of feet away.

There was probably more, but it was lost in her startled shriek. She jumped back into the entryway, pulled the door closed with a bang, and flipped the lock.

After a few moments, as the pounding of her heart slowed, she inched toward the door. She almost shrieked again when a round, concerned-looking face appeared at the window.

"You okay in there?" the man called through the glass.

It was definitely not the voice she had heard a moment before.

"Yes, I'm okay," she said loudly. "Who are you?"

"Tony. From the pizza place. Are you that psychic lady?"

She flipped the lock and eased the door open, her foot planted behind it to prevent any uninvited entry. "Yes. Ann Kinnear."

"Pleased to meet you." He was about the same height as Ann, but about twice as wide, and all muscle. His neck was a mere suggestion, the muscle running straight from his earlobes to the tips of his shoulders. The bulk of his biceps cantilevered his arms out from his barrel-like chest. Each of his thighs was the size of Ann's waist. He held out his hand and she shook it through the narrow opening, grateful that he kept his grip light. "I heard Mrs. Gorman hired you. Poor lady, what a thing to go through."

"Yes, it's pretty unimaginable," said Ann, relaxing her hold on the door.

"Guess it was even worse for Trina. Probably feels responsible, in a way, although of course it wasn't her fault. Just bad luck who she fell in with. And then fell out with, I guess."

"Yes."

"And then to be up there for ten minutes with him—just the two of them and those bodies on the floor. Gives me the heebie-jeebies to think about it." He shuddered. "But I guess they're both luckier than the others who were here that night." He shook his head. "You okay? I thought I heard a scream."

"I saw a mouse," said Ann.

"Mouse?" said Tony, his face blanching. "Where?"

Ann waved vaguely in the direction of the parking lot. "It was headed that way."

Tony shook his head. "Little bastards." He glanced at her. "Pardon my French."

"No problem."

"Well, if everything's okay, I better get back." He turned toward the pizza shop.

"Hey," said Ann, stepping out onto the sidewalk, "were you here that night?"

"Sure was," said Tony. "Just about this time." He glanced at his watch. "Well, a little earlier. Fortunately we didn't have any customers right then—it was just me and Freddy in the shop—but I heard the shooting and screaming. I locked the door and turned off all the lights so it would look like no one was home, and called 911.

A couple of cop cars got here fast, but they had to wait for backup. About ten minutes after the first shooting, while they were still trying to figure out what to do—and trying to talk to the guy—there was one more shot, and they went in."

"That was when he killed himself?"

"Yeah. I say good riddance. Saved all those poor families from having to go through a trial."

They were silent for a moment, then Ann said, "Thank for checking on me."

"Sure," said Tony. He hesitated. "You, uh … you seen anybody? Heard anybody? You know, anybody dead?"

"Not here," she replied, although she was pretty sure that wasn't true.

"Well, good luck," he said. "Stop by for a slice when you're done. On the house."

They shook hands again and Ann watched him disappear into the pizza shop.

She looked carefully up and down the walkway, then said, "Hello?"

"You're not going to scream again, are you?" said the voice.

She did let out a little yelp, then tried to disguise it by coughing into her fist.

"Who are you?" she asked.

"You're looking for Alan Gorman, right?"

"Yes."

"Let me in and I'll talk. I have lots to say."

"Great." She started through the door, relieved that she would have something to report to Miranda.

"You'll need to hold the door open for me," he said from behind her.

"Really?"

"Yes, really."

She eased the door open and stood back. She tried to sense some movement, but could perceive nothing. In a moment, though, she heard the voice from the entryway.

"Okay, I'm in. Let's go upstairs."

Leaving the door unlocked on the slight possibility that Miranda would decide to show up, Ann climbed the stairs slowly, anxious not to walk into the space of a spirit she couldn't see. If he couldn't pass through a closed door, could she bump into him? The question was a new one for her, since she had never encountered a spirit who seemed to be bound by the rules of the physical world. She had also never encountered a spirit whom she could hear so clearly, but see not at all.

She got to the top of the stairs and looked around, hopeful that the bright fluorescent lights of the studio might reveal something, but the room appeared empty.

"Alan?"

"I'm here."

Fortunately, the voice wasn't right next to her, otherwise she might have risked a start and a tumble back down the stairs. It sounded like he was standing near the line of folding chairs.

"How are you doing?" she asked after a moment.

"Well, you know," he said, a trace of a smile in his voice. "Dead."

"Yeah." She moved toward the chairs. "Why can't I see you?"

"Haven't a clue. Why can you hear me? No one else can."

"It's an ability I have."

She sat down on a chair a couple of yards away from where the voice was emanating.

"Miranda wants to talk with you," she said. "She's been here with me every night, but she has a migraine and couldn't come tonight. Can I call her and tell her you're here?"

"No," he said. "I don't have anything to say to her."

They sat in silence for a minute, then Ann said, "You said you had lots to say …"

She perceived no indication of movement, but when he spoke next, his voice came from near the door to the office.

"Have you ever been in love?"

Ann hesitated. "Yes."

"Now?"

"No."

"What happened?"

How much was she required to reveal about her personal life as part of a consulting engagement? At least it wasn't likely he would be gossiping about it with anyone else.

"He didn't believe I could do what I do," she said.

"Talking to dead people?"

"Sensing them. He thought I needed psychiatric help."

He snorted out a brief laugh. "Sometimes people think the damnedest thinks."

"Yes."

"When I fell in love," he continued after a moment, "I fell in love with the whole woman. Not part of her. I didn't hope in the back of my mind that I could fix her flaws. As far as I was concerned, there were no flaws."

Ann hoped Alan was talking about Miranda, otherwise the debrief of the evening's events with her client was going to be somewhat awkward.

"You're an insightful man," she said. "She was a lucky woman."

"Well, I thought so."

"She obviously loved you, too," she said. "I think it's safe to say she still loves you, since she hired me to communicate with you."

"We were together for so long. We were perfect together. We could finish each other's sentences. And the dancing—the dancing was sublime."

"The rumba?"

He laughed. "All of them."

A half minute ticked by, then she heard the whir of the CD player spinning up.

"Care to dance?" He was right in front of her.

She stood and reluctantly held out her hand.

He took it and pulled her toward him.

"Have you ever danced?" he asked.

"Not real dancing."

"It's easy if you just follow," he said, and she jumped when she felt his hand on the small of her back. "Relax," he said soothingly.

He began to move, and to move her with him, smoothly correcting her stumbles, and she realized that the song wasn't a rumba, but rather the sultry strains of a tango.

She caught occasional glimpses of herself in the fragments of mirror still clinging to the wall, the vision of herself moving with an invisible partner freakish and unsettling. But there was something seductive, too, about the experience—as she listened to the music and she began to understand the movements and rhythm of the dance, she did relax into it.

After a minute, he spoke softly. "You know, when you make a commitment to someone, it's for life. It doesn't matter if you have a ring to prove it, or if it's just a promise between the two of you. It's forever. Until death do you part."

"Sometimes not even then," she said gamely.

His arm tightened around her waist. "Exactly. Exactly! That's what I want to tell her."

"I can tell her for you."

They were moving more easily now, and he laughed—a light, gay sound. "I'm so glad I found you." He twirled her out, and then pulled her back against his body. "You're a natural."

She laughed uncomfortably. "Not so much. Are you sure you don't want me to call Miranda?"

The push when it came was so unexpected that she went sprawling onto the ground.

"No, I don't want you calling Miranda," he said, his voice taut with anger. "Why do you women always have to do that? Why do you always have to bring someone else into it?"

"I don't know what you're talking about!"

"Miranda. Travis. *Trina and Travis*, for God's sake. It sounds like a bad sitcom."

Ann felt the blood drain from her face. "Who are you?"

"Who do you think I am?"

She hesitated. "Edward?"

"That's me," he said, and a hysterical lilt had crept into his voice.

So the visitor to the studio wasn't Miranda's husband. It was Edward Lester, the man who a month before had climbed the stairs to the studio and raked the room and its occupants with gunfire before turning the gun on himself.

"I thought you were Alan Gorman," she said weakly.

"I never said that. You assumed."

She was silent.

In a moment, he spoke again. "Trina and I had it all. We had the studio. We had the competitions. We had a shot at the big titles. And, most important, we had each other. And then she decided she didn't want it. I want to know why she didn't want it."

Ann began to stand up.

"Sit down!" he said sharply.

She lowered herself back onto the floor, her heart pounding.

"What do you want me to do about it?"

"I've got to talk to Trina. She hasn't come to the studio on her own, and I can't go to her—it seems like I can't leave here. And even if she did come, I don't know if she'd be able to hear me. But," he said, closer, "you could get her to come, and if she can't hear me, you can tell her what I'm saying."

"I don't even know how to get in touch with her," she said, struggling to keep her voice steady. "She went into hiding."

"You could find her if you wanted to."

"I don't think I could. And even if I could, I wouldn't try to bring her back here."

"Why not?"

Ann paused a beat, but anger began to push aside her alarm. "You killed her partner and five of her students."

"That little bastard deserved it."

"Nobody deserves that!" she shot back, her own voice rising. "And the other ones were just innocent bystanders. In fact, it seems like one of them had exactly the kind of relationship with his wife that you wish you had with Trina. Because his widow is paying me to sit in this room and try to communicate—"

Her head rocked back with an invisible slap.

"Shut up!" he yelled.

She scuttled back on her hands and feet.

"No, wait!" An invisible hand clamped onto her upper arm. Hard. "Please!" She could hear tears beneath his strident voice. "I need you to bring Trina to me."

"Let me go!" she yelled.

"You don't know what it's like to be powerless," he yelled back. "If you won't help me, I'll show you! I'll make you as powerless as I am! I'll—"

"Rats!" she screamed.

"What the hell?"

"Tony! Rats!" She twisted her arm, and his grip tightened further.

He grabbed her other arm and shook her, her head snapping back and forth. "Stop it! Stop it! I need you to help me, I need you to bring Trina to me!"

"Tony! Rats!"

The door at the bottom of the stairs banged open.

"Rats?" His squawk echoed up the stairwell.

"There are rats up here, Tony! Rats!"

"Come on out of there," Tony yelled as he pounded up the steps. "Rats is nothing to be fooling around with!"

Ann felt the grip on her arms relax fractionally, and she wrenched herself free and scrambled to her feet just as Tony reached the top of the stairs.

"Let's get out of here," she gasped.

Tony took her arm. "You okay? Where are they?" he asked, his gaze shooting around the seemingly empty studio.

"Back there. Let's get out of here."

With Tony's hand steadying her, she stumbled down the stairs. At the bottom, she turned.

She couldn't see him, but she could sense him, standing at the top of the stairs, that dark, handsome man who had spun Trina

Hochmann across a dance floor, and had later gunned down her new partner and a roomful of students.

"Please," Edward Lester called down the stairs, almost sobbing. "Please, I need to talk to her, and you're the only one who can help me."

"I'll call the exterminator tomorrow," said Tony as he led Ann out onto the sidewalk. "Rats—I can't believe it."

*   *   *   *   *

The exterminator searched the studio the next day, and reported no sign of rats.

Mike Kinnear notified Miranda Gorman that, in Ann's professional opinion, if Alan were still around to be contacted, he would have shown up by now, and ended the engagement.

Ann returned to West Chester, her shirt sleeve covering the bruises on her arms—the clear impression of four fingers and a thumb.

Caitlyn Gorman rescheduled her wedding for the following year, with a reduction in headcount of seven.

And three months later, a new business, Tony's Toning and Muscle Center, opened in the space previously occupied by Sentimental Journey Dance Studio.

Read more Ann Kinnear stories in Matty Dalrymple's novels.

A GAL NAMED HARRIET

There once was a gal named Harriet

Who traveled by way of a chariot

Too much bounce as he sped

So she chopped off his head

Now the driver is forced to carry it

MANUFACTURING DYSTOPIA
Lanny Larcinese

Friday, June 23, 1967

Sally Kavner's father Herb had said all along something was about to blow, and when it did, the city would empty faster than a high colonic. She thought of this as she watched the maitre d' escort Detroit's elite to their tables following the concert at the Ford Auditorium, her smiling demeanor, like so much else in the city, concealing something.

A man in the party of four trailing behind the maître d' turned and gave her a surreptitious wink as he passed Sally's hostess station. The others paid scant attention to the stunning, copper-haired young woman in the black dress and pearls also in his party, instead listening to the winking man hold forth that though the Detroit Symphony's Maestro had personally known Stravinsky, Sixten Ehrling still could not conduct the *Rite of Spring* as well as Paul Paray.

Sally deflected the unwanted attention with a pasted-on hostess smile.

More crap. She'd rather be banging on her Olivetti, setting the keys on fire with stories about the city's hypocritical *noblesse oblige,* about how blue-bloods pontificated social ideals and pretentiously debated classical music in rococo rooms like the DeVille Room of the Book Cadillac Hotel, then retreated to gated enclaves as the great unwashed struggled to make it through another day, hatred crackling like bacon in smoky oil, their fuse awaiting an insouciantly tossed match. *Motor City Now* might even let her do a series.

MCN was a tiny, free weekly with wide circulation in the city's black ghettos. That the so-called racial renaissance was an illusion echoed loudly around *MCN*'s hallways, while the big dailies pandered to limousine liberals with booster stories about black progress: *Billions in Great Society Money for Neighborhoods,* crowed the headlines of the *News* and *Free Press*, along with editorials thanking God Earl Warren was still Chief Justice.

But something was seriously amiss in the land—an *Alice in Wonderland* quality—heightened agitation from burgeoning Viet Nam war demonstrators; the grim voices of Dr. King and the Black Panthers; Age of Aquarius peace and equality marches; and on the very cover of the cognoscenti's sacred writ—*New York Review of Books*—how to assemble a Molotov cocktail. Sally and her dad, a volunteer at the ACLU, had watched the social unrest with alarm and talked about it all through her journalism studies at Wayne State. Buffalo Springfield had it right, *"There's something happening here, what it is ain't exactly clear…"*

She scanned the reservation book to see whose name the party's reservation was under. *Roy Jackson.* Was he the one who winked at her? He seemed to be in charge, at least the most arrogant. The city's movers and shakers were fodder for good stories, especially if they had something juicy to leak. She reached for the phone and called Ricky Trupiano, the Book Cadillac's parking valet supervisor who could get more skinny than the FBI. "Trupe, me. Get me the license number of the party of four that just came in. Yeah, them. And rifle the glove box, see if there's anything in the car I can use."

She returned her attention to the dining room's genteel hum. Her constant feeling that something was about to happen caused her to frequently scan the Savile Row and bejeweled Givenchy patrons engaged in gay, animated conversation as tuxedoed *sommeliers* displayed wine labels for scrutiny or waiters drew out velvet chairs or served food with a flourish and carved it or spooned it from impeccable sets of silver service. She just *knew* there were a hundred stories under all the smugness. Better yet, was it too much to ask that some blue-haired lady faint into a bowl of lobster bisque or captain of industry have wine thrown in his face?

The tap on her shoulder broke her wishful reverie. She turned and smiled reflexively at a young man. He was glancing over at the window table where Roy Jackson's husky voice went on and on, dominating that corner of the room while others in his party looked at him with wide-eyed affirmation and the fixed smiles of people knowing who picked up the check.

"Aren't you Sally Kavner?" the young man asked, turning his attention back toward her. Thirtyish. Some premature gray. Soft-spoken. Sleeves of his camel blazer a little too long. Black shoes looked plastic rather than the Gucci loafers that typically slid lightly over the red carpet of the DeVille Room.

"I'm Sally, but I don't give autographs," she quipped. "Table for one?"

"Not really. I didn't come to eat. I only wanted to meet you and introduce myself. My name is Marc Davis. Sergeant Marc Davis, DPD."

Was this an undercover thing? about a customer? the restaurant? something she wrote? Didn't she catch him looking over at the Roy Jackson table?

"You write for *Motor City Now* don't you?" he said. "That Sally Kavner?"

"I am."

"Can we have lunch or something sometime? I'd like to tell you about my work," he said, alleviating the tension that set up house in her shoulders when she smelled a story.

"Well lunch might be good. Not too sure about the something," she said with a laugh and seductive smile.

"That's great. How can I reach you?"

"Send out an APB. Kidding! How about I call you."

He gave her a card. Police contacts were useful no matter what this was about.

Sergeant Marc Davis. Internal Affairs. Headquarters Building, Beaubien Street. She smiled at him and put it in her purse as he turned and left. She always hoped that her part-time gig at the Book might lead to something more important than the buck-an-hour wage, but what the *hell* was this about?

Tuesday, June 27

The next morning, her call went directly to the switchboard of police headquarters. "Patrolman Hankowsky," barked the answerer. She asked for Sergeant Davis in Internal Affairs, but hung up as her call was being transferred. Davis was IA okay, but what had he wanted? Maybe something she could sink her teeth into. He could have gone to the big dailies but didn't. It better not be some kind of come-on. No, that wasn't his vibe. He had something. She had run it by her editor at *MCN*. "Milk it," he said. "Maybe it's big." It might also perk up her dad who was sick, the outcome of his stroke uncertain. He would be so proud if she broke an important story.

When she finally spoke with Marc she kept it casual though his conspiratorial tone made her curiosity itch yet more. They agreed to meet Thursday.

Something. He must have *something*.

She went to her closet and eyed her wardrobe. Nothing fancy for the rendezvous. Keep it simple. Jeans and a top. Pony tail. Light make-up. Put him at ease. Maybe her brown, pointy-toed boots. They had a nice heel. Make her taller. Look him in the eye. Take his measure.

Thursday, June 29

He was already there when she arrived at Ziggy's Pierogi Factory in Hamtramck, a Polish enclave and virtual annex to the muscular and cavernous Dodge Main Assembly plant across the street. He was in uniform and looked intense. He stood to greet her, pulled out her chair, then sat.

"I love Hamtramck," she opened with. "It's so vital. We aren't Polish, but many of my people were from Poland." Unsaid was, *but suffered pogroms and didn't make it through the Holocaust.* She was never comfortable in the little city of modest, bungalow-styled homes entirely surrounded by the City of Detroit—its street life happy as a polka but its favored duck-blood soup symbolic of the mother country's sad history and oppressive present. You had to be blind not to see that beneath Detroit's Midwestern friendliness and industrial might was a cancerous, ulcerated underbelly.

"Are you a native Detroiter?"

"Fourth generation cop." His smile looked forced, not fake but trying hard. Whatever he had to get off his chest seemed urgent and small talk not his game.

"So why this meeting, Sergeant? Which of my pieces did you like in *Motor City Now?*"

"A few of them, but I looked you up because of what I saw between the lines, except I…I…" She looked at him expectantly. "I…I didn't know you'd be so pretty." He looked down and blushed. She was charmed he would say something clearly not easy for him. It wasn't flirtatious, but a naïve forthrightness. "You wouldn't say that if you saw me with no makeup, Marc."

"I would!" he said eagerly.

"Thank you. It's flattering." She touched his hand. "What did you see between the lines?"

"Honesty, for one. The article about redlining opened my eyes."

"Everybody knows what goes on. Some don't want to admit it."

"That's what I wanted to talk about…"

She let the matter trail off. She sat looking at him, saying nothing, waiting for the awkward silence to cause his words to spew.

He finally decided to speak.

"I'm really a street cop. I love the street, catching bad guys, but I've been kicked upstairs to a desk job"

"Why a desk job?"

"I feel like I can trust you from your writing, but I want your word…"

"Take it to the bank, but…?"

"Okay, then, the reason they put me in IA is a keep-your-enemies-closer deal. I get jerk-off assignments like cops sleeping in cars or raising their voice or something. I write up their version. My reports to Lieutenant Steiglitz get scrubbed before they go to the Captain. It's how they whitewash stuff for public consumption."

This wasn't news. Maybe it was a come-on after all. She opened her purse and put on her sunglasses. "All bureaucracies are a bitch." She pushed her chair out. "Thanks for the coffee Marc, but I'm not your girl, you need to talk to Personnel."

"Yeah, but there's more." She sat down and pushed her glasses onto her forehead.

"More what?"

"What they know but aren't doing anything about."

"Marc, do you know what blue-balls are?"

"We're right on the brink."

"Brink of what?"

"Do you mind if we order something. I'm starved."

"Sure."

He told her about the Clean-up Squads—burly detectives who pulled black people off the streets and worked them over in alleys, often beating them senseless.

"Police brutality is the best kept secret since the Bay of Pigs invasion," she said.

"There's more. You know the riots in Atlanta last year? Word on the force is that the FBI is investigating that anarchists are behind it."

"Why, to justify the happy-talk of all the Motor City amity?" she said. She repeated the mantra, "Liberal mayor, Great Society money, et cetera. Do you have specifics that say otherwise?"

"There's Detective Chaney and a guy named Roy Jackson. I saw Jackson at the Book when I stopped in to introduce myself to you."

Finally! She pulled a notebook and pencil from her purse. "Spell."

"C-H-A-N-E-Y, D-E-R-E-K. One of our black detectives. Clean as a bar of soap. He frisked some white kid four months ago up on Harper near Chalmers and brings the kid in for questioning. Later, IA gets a complaint that Chaney stuck his .38 up the kid's rectum and caused serious tissue damage. Turns out the kid is the son of some VIP, this Roy Jackson. You don't need me to spell Jackson."

"The kid's name?"

"George, aka Georgiecheeks. His father Roy is General Counsel for the Ford Dealers Association. He's screaming for Chaney's head but wants it kept quiet. Except IA discovers the kid is queer and a former boyfriend tells one of our guys it's how he got injured, rough sex I guess, but they're burying it so they can deliver Chaney's head up to this big-shot Jackson."

She remembered… last week…at the Book. Swanky party of four with a loudmouth host who droned on about the know-nothing Maestro and paid the check. She had asked Trupe to root around his car then forgot to follow up when she didn't hear back.

"Can I talk to Chaney?"

"Not yet. I don't want anybody to know I'm talking to you. You don't know my people."

"Why would they object? Investigating cops is what you do. I can be of help."

"Yeah, sometimes I do it on my own. I tailed Jackson in the past, it's why I recognized him when I saw him in the restaurant where you work. But my people won't like that I'm trying to help Derek. Even he doesn't know. But it's not right that he's being hosed." Marc stirred his coffee so strenuously it splashed over and filled the saucer. When he set the spoon down, Sally saw his hand was shaking. "It'll get ugly."

Thursday, July 6

Sally and Trupe weren't scheduled for duty at the Book until Friday evening. She left a message for him at his other job at Stevie's Limousine. He called her back from the airport.

"I left a message for you but you never called back," he said.

"I didn't get it. Did you learn anything about that party I asked you to check on?"

"Yeah. I didn't park the car, Phil did, but here's the scoop...Lincoln Continental convertible, red, 340 horses, 462 cubes—

"Trupe, please?"

"Okay. The registration was in the glove box. Guy's name is Roy Jackson. He uses Esquire. Got your pencil?" He gave her Jackson's addresses: Lahser Road in Bloomfield Hills and Ford HQ in Dearborn. "Seems he's also involved in some flap with DPD. Lenny Goldblum, a bail bondsman I know knows a guy in the police union who mentioned it, but I couldn't get any more. What's this guy's story?"

"Don't know yet. Still lookin' into it."

"Let me know if it's anything juicy. I can use it in trade."

"You should sell rugs in a Turkish bazaar."

"I think I did in another life. Okay, Sal, gotta go meet my arrival."

She drove straight to Bloomfield Hills to scout, maybe steal some mail. She parked near Jackson's wrought-iron gate and wall of lilacs to watch for comings and goings. As she waited she puzzled over how she could get to the front door. Maybe it was easier to catch him at his work under the guise of a puff-piece, connect dots between him and the DPD, maybe the Prosecutor's office, maybe higher.

As she reached into her handbag for her notebook, she was startled by a sudden banging on her window, causing half of the purse's contents to fly out. A Bloomfield Hills policeman motioned for her to lower the window. She looked into her mirror. She hadn't seen the squad car parked behind her with its reds and blues flashing. How long had it been there?

"Are you broken down, Ma'am?" the policeman asked.

"No, officer, I just pulled over to look for some things in my purse."

He took her license and registration back to his car, then returned a minute later.

"Can you pull onto Woodward Avenue and do whatever you need to do?"

"Sure. Have I done anything wrong?"

"No, Ma'am, just move away from here."

Saturday, July 8

Detective Derek Chaney was a large man with small, well-manicured hands and a thunderous voice. Divorced. Father ex-military; mother an elementary school teacher, both deceased. Sally met him at his apartment near the Greyhound Station at Trumbull and Porter where he lived with a girlfriend, Janice Roberts. He wanted to meet while Janice was at work. "This whole incident gets her uptight," he said. The apartment was impeccably clean and still smelled of Lysol. "Not much else to do," he had said.

They went out to the porch and talked. He was in khakis and a blue oxford-cloth shirt. Sally thought he dressed well for a cop on suspension pending an investigation. Showed he still cared. She kept him talking about his youth, about growing up on Twelfth near Clairmont.

"I know white folks feel unsafe around here," he said, "but if any of 'em spent a Friday night at Sawyer's to hear Yusef or Charles Mingus, well, nobody cares what color you are. Only price of admission is you love music." She wanted to buy into it, but no wishful thinking could sanitize the constant, ugly mayhem that terrorized white people as well as black, sometimes just to steal their sneaks. Often, worse.

"Was it a good place to grow up?" she asked.

"Even though Dad had been military, he was out by the time I came along. I'll tell you this though, you had to be able to take care of yourself."

"Meaning…?"

"Unpleasantness. Blind pigs all over. I stayed away from it but it went on."

Blind pig, local parlance for private after-hours drinking places and shooting galleries— vice dens to cops who raided them—social clubs for the locals. "Sooner or later somebody tries to take your spot, or your money, or your woman, then's when the cannons go off and you better know how to take care of yourself," Chaney said.

"What made you become a cop?"

"There's law and there's order. I felt like I knew the difference better than most."

Stripped of bias, most cops did, but that was a huge caveat in Detroit. As long as victims suffered in silence, the orchestra played, and Dungeness crab was plentiful, who gave a damn?

"Have you? Made a difference?"

"Not enough. When I made detective they sent me to white neighborhoods on the East Side, an integration image thing, wantin' to show we all just brothers."

"It hasn't worked out so well, based on the Jackson case."

"You have to keep this confidential…if word gets out I'll deny I said anything…"

"It's what we do, Derek, we protect sources."

"Marc Davis says you're stand-up..."

"I want to help."

"A lot goes on," he said.

"Why don't you start with George Jackson?"

"Okay, well, him and another guy were in a four-seater Thunderbird in a dark parking lot behind the Via Appia restaurant up on Harper Avenue. Me and my partner, Henry Abbot, are in an unmarked car. It's two a.m. when we spot the T-Bird. We park a distance away and Henry sneaks up and shines his light into the car and yells, 'Police!' Inside the car, two guys are having sex. When the light shines on them Henry goes around to the driver's side. One of the men bolts out the rear passenger side, and get this, no pants, and runs off."

"Geez, was he wearing shoes?"

"I don't remember, but Henry takes off after him. Now, Henry looks like the Pillsbury Doughboy, so I'm not optimistic he'll catch the guy. I have my hand on my piece and yell for the other guy to get out. It was George Jackson. My partner is gone for a good while. The guy gave him the slip and Henry tried to find him, thinking he couldn't be too far away without pants, or so Henry said. Seemed like he was gone a real long time."

"What did George Jackson say?"

"He tried to talk me down. Said they weren't doing anything wrong. Said could I give him a break, that if his father found out he'd be severely punished, that his father was a prominent man. Said I'd be better off if I let him go. He was really afraid."

"Why didn't you? Let him go I mean. Doesn't sound like a major deal."

"I found powder and a needle in the car. Looked like heroin. I cuffed him, put him in our car, and waited until Henry got back. He finally came back empty handed."

"Then what?"

"Took Jackson to the station. We're grilling him about the other guy and the dope. In the middle of the interrogation, the Lieutenant comes in and tells us the kid's lawyer is out front. I find out later that the kid alleged that I stuck my piece up his rectum. Maybe he didn't want his father to know he's homosexual. Now the FBI is involved."

"Why? The arrest was routine, wasn't it? Even the brutality claim, right?"

"The kid's father must have pulled strings. He wants to establish that I abused the kid. His allegation is racial animus, stuff like that. But the Department is resisting. It doesn't want press about a black cop harming a white kid. So Jackson keeps going up the ladder and I'm on the bottom rung."

"Didn't your people find out from someone that he got hurt from rough sex?"

"Yeah, but the father won't hear of it. So, now, they can't find the kid who gave them that story. They can't find their notes. They can't find shit."

Sunday, July 9

Sally cruised a few dozen blocks around the Twelfth Street ghetto. She eyed the small shops—shoes, clothes, furniture, bakeries, storefront churches—the usual suspicious looks and thrum of racial antipathy silent behind steel-shuttered doors. Up and down Linwood was a wall of poorly maintained apartment buildings. Strings of worn-out sneakers hung from telephone wires above the tiny tornadoes of wind-blown litter on the decrepit sidewalks below. Dressed-up church ladies in fancy hats strolled down the street, some holding babies as they walked, some with freshly scrubbed kids in ill-fitting suits, running and cavorting ahead of them.

Sally pulled in front of the Twelfth Street address where Derek Chaney was reared. She rang all six bells, two responded. She told each she was doing a profile of Derek, one of the few black detectives on the DPD, and needed to find out what kind of child he had been. Did they know him back then? Did they feel better that the DPD was hiring more Negroes? Yes, they remembered Derek. Yes, they would like more black police, "If you po'," said one, "white po-lice treat you like shit, and they ain't no call for that. We fed up."

Wednesday, July 12

Her press credential allowed access to the morgues at both the *News* and the *Free Press*. The "racial incident" files were multiple volumes. Sally shook her head in disbelief as the story over time unfolded. Many of the articles involved vandalism by white people in black neighborhoods, or colored people assaulted by white people, seldom the reverse, and racism frequently insinuated even in the absence of evidence. A lot of the reporting was about ham-handed policing, calls for mayoral action, and we-cannot-allow-this-here editorials, their tone glibly underscoring victimhood . It didn't compute. It was pseudo-appeasement and she wondered if it was in part the basis for so much delusional self-satisfaction by the city fathers at the expense of real progress and goodwill. She put the material back. This wasn't right. Newspaper-world was different from real life, and her stomach roiled in frustration that the city was a powder keg and Mayor Cavanaugh, instead of being another JFK as was his press, was instead a snickering Wile E. Coyote lighting a wooden match.

She took her notes to Marc. "Look at this pandering bullshit. I'm waiting to see if they're gonna say the riot in Newark is outside agitators."

"Yeah, and when the black people really *are* the victims, I have yet to see any cop punished for brutality. Except for Derek. By the way, word is that he's going to be dismissed and prosecuted. I don't know if he knows yet.

"How is he supposed to defend himself?" Sally asked.

"The Fraternal Order of Police will help, but he'd get more help if he was white."

"The people down at Twelfth & Linwood talk about him like he's Hans Christian Andersen," she said.

"What kind of relationships did he tell you he has in the squad room?" Marc asked.

"Cordial."

"That's bullshit! Most cops are like brothers to each other. In this environment 'cordial' is a left-handed compliment and means you're crap. I don't wonder if his partner didn't do it on purpose, the night of the Jackson incident, being gone so long looking for the other perp, leaving Derek to handle things without a backup. Maybe it was part of a set up."

"Henry Abbot is white?"

"Yep, and never wanted to partner with Derek."

Wednesday, July 19

It was hot for a Detroit July, ninety-four degrees on the day Derek Chaney barricaded himself in his apartment and was stormed by the FBI and DPD's Special Reaction Team. They took him down after he fired on them from a third floor window instead of giving himself up to be placed under arrest for the denial of civil rights, sodomy, battery, and host of other charges surrounding the detainment of one George Jackson.

Derek was flat-out assassinated. Sally knew it. So did Marc.

Marc had called Sally as soon as it came over the radio. By the time she got there Derek Chaney was dead, his body not yet brought out. Three hundred or so people had stood behind the perimeter and watched the take-down. Sally tried to interview them between their angry shouts. She counted ten blue and whites, a couple dozen cops in uniform, and a dozen in plain clothes with shields dangling around their necks, all ignoring the angry and indignant shouts from the crowd. Bottles not thrown at the police were smashed to the ground—sharp, glinting shards as piercing as the icy glares of the still-gathering crowd. Four more wagonloads of police in full riot gear arrived and formed a phalanx between the crowd and scene investigators. Sally tried to get interviews. She changed her tack and said, "I knew Detective Chaney, did you know him? What can you tell me about him?"

"What he do the whole army come after him?" many wanted to know.

When the crowd became suddenly quiet she turned and saw Derek's body being wheeled out on the gurney, blood soaking through the sheets. The crowd moaned collectively. The shouting got louder and fist-shaking more angry. Young men threw stones and bottles toward the coroner's van as it pulled away. The riot police charged, wrestled them to the ground, and cuffed them. More bottles flew. The police retreated back, then formed a V-shaped wedge and again charged into the crowd swinging batons, dividing it and yelling for everybody to go home, the show was over.

Sally and Marc went straight to Cross's Tavern on Adams Street facing Grand Circus Park and drank themselves silly. They sat at the bar, side by side, occasionally saying things like, "Man," or, "I can't believe it," or, "Shit," or, "This place is so fucked up," the pall too heavy to curse the city that allowed it to happen, caused it to happen.

"I feel like I'm stuck in a Hieronymus Bosch painting," she slurred after four Stroh's and numerous rounds of Old Hickory.

"Who's he?"

"You don't wanna know."

"All the guys at headquarters were saying stuff like good riddance," Marc said.

"I wanted a story," she said, "but this is awful. I don't think I can touch it. I'd rather be upside-down in a barrel of worms."

He looked at her, weaving on his barstool. "Don't give up on this," he slurred. "We can change the narrative on the whole mess."

"How, Marc? What can we do? Can't you see how deep this goes?"

"I thought you told me you had your father's never-quit."

"What, like Superman? What did it do for my dad? It put him in the hospital with a fucking stroke." Marc had no answer he could pull together. They ordered another round.

"You know," he finally said, "I looked you up because when I read your stuff, I… I… dunno, I saw something, somebody 'd stick their neck out with me, somebody 'd look up and see hope instead of a guillotine."

"How're we gonna keep a lid on? How?" she asked.

"'s easy, don't worry about lid, do what's right."

"I need a break," she said, "I need time to think. I need to pee. I'm gonna go home now and hug my cat and cry. Sunday I'm gonna go to Ann Arbor and see my dad in the hospital, talk to him about things. Maybe he'll have some advice. Or something." She slid off the stool with one hand on the bar to steady herself.

"I'll drive you. You're too fucked up to drive."

"Right, she grinned," and you're Bill Wilson. How about this, how about we share a cab?"

"Okay, but would you put me up? I'm way too messed up to make it home."

"Yeah, the couch."

"What, you don't want comfort?"

She understood. She understood his need to know there was still love in the world, his need to be anchored to human touch and warmth in the midst of a rabid sucking maelstrom. Just for one night.

"Okay. C'mon over."

Sunday, July 23

Sally left the city at seven-thirty a.m. to visit her father and arrived in Ann Arbor at nine fifteen. She followed the long green line through the maze of the Hospital of the University of Michigan to the Neurology wing. An aide was feeding him lunch. The brutal sagging asymmetry of the left side of his face looked like a waxen bust left too near a radiator. She pulled a chair to his bedside and solemnly nodded to her mother who sat on the other side of the bed.

"Hi Daddy. How do you feel today?" He could only grunt and nod. Soup and spittle leaked out of the side of his mouth. Sally looked at her mother who was holding his hand. Her mother smiled stoically. "Your dad's doing really well," she said, with the kind of hospital happy-talk intended to boost the spirits of the sick yet bear the crushing weight of fear and despair. Sally sat quietly until he was fed, and watched her once-strong and proud father, a man of ideals and fire in the belly, reduced to the dependency of a baby.

"I need your advice," Sally finally said. Droopy eyelid and all, his eyes met hers with the same dependable gaze that saw her through so many crises in her young life, which she long ago learned was his needing to help as much as her needing it from him. She went on to unfold the Roy Jackson story and Derek Chaney's death, that she was stymied as to where to go from there. When she was done he couldn't speak, could voice no advice. Instead he pushed his tray table aside and grunted a loud, forceful grunt sending soup and spittle spraying onto her blouse, and with fire in his eyes, held a tightly clenched fist up to her and speared it into the air, then grunted more loudly yet and thrust the fist upward again, this time higher. Her eyes welled with tears. She looked at him and said, "I won't, Daddy, not ever."

As she headed back to Detroit on the Ford Expressway the golden sun on her face bathed her in welcome respite from grief and frustration. The visit had quelled much of her depression about the city she loved so dearly, and in the car's cocoon she felt more able to think, inspired that her father's rabid spirit still stirred inside its broken vessel and inside her. But she still felt like she bore the weight of the world. The times were so troubling: Anti-Viet Nam demonstrations, riots in Atlanta and Newark—so much chaos giving birth. To what? And her home town, the town of her home, teetering on the brink, its Panglossian movers and shakers deaf to crying voices, the flickering needle of their moral compass leading them to the eighth circle of hell reserved for frauds.

Yet Detroit would remain standing, or so it seemed. After all, she and her father and maybe Marc took their cue from JFK—idealists without illusions.

Sure the city had its share of hypocrites, and who knew how many victim constituencies spawned demagogues fomenting discontent or worse, anarchy. Even the Detroit dailies had agendas, subtly puncturing journalism's ideals like a screw through a steel-belted radial. Except their mind-control games gambled with lives and they seemed incapable of asking: what if we're wrong? But Detroit was still the Motor City, a robust town of a million and a half, and she and her father and Marc and people like them would help clean it up with goodwill shouted from its mountain top of problems and with hearts the size of billboards.

She assumed traffic on the expressway was thin because it was Sunday. The sound of sirens disrupted her thoughts. She looked up above the embankment of the sunken expressway and saw a plume of smoke and heard the clang of fire engines.

She resumed her reverie. The problems were formidable. Look at Marc, like many Detroiters of goodwill, heart in the right place but trapped in a system. Maybe hope was all there was.

Then she heard more sirens and tried to see over the inclined berm.

Another fire—huge—judging from the giant column of billowing smoke.

She exited the freeway and parked in front of her apartment building. More sirens in the distance. She was amused recalling the difficulty she and Marc had a few nights ago, drunkenly trying to get the key in the door. He passed out before he got lucky. That was okay, she covered his naked body and lay beside him, her arm around his chest, a lifeline for them both.

She threw her purse and keys onto the table and turned on the radio. A blind pig had been raided by the police during the night and a crowd had gathered. "Jesus, again?" she moaned. She turned the volume down as she picked up the phone. It was three p.m. She hadn't eaten since yesterday. Her head pounded. She was exhausted and famished. She called Gaetano's for pizza. The phone rang a half dozen times before anybody picked up. Busy this time of day on a summer Sunday?

"Yes, I'd like a small pizza delivered please. Pepperoni."

"Are you insane lady? We're closed. Don't you know there's a riot going on? The whole fuckin' town is on fire."

A KNIFE DISAPPEARED

A knife disappeared from the kitchen

As the staff was in the midst of a switchin'

The lights all went black

The knife found its way back

In someone's melon, it ended up pitched in

HOME OF THE FRIDAY FAJITA FIESTA

Tom Joyce

"Don't touch it, I implore you," the old man said. "It is an ancient tome, full of eldritch secrets that might drive one insane with sheer terror!"

The waitress, a petite young woman in a striped shirt and suspenders, interrupted.

"Welcome to T.J. O'Shaunessy's Family Food and Fun Emporium, home of the Friday Fajita Fiesta! I'd like to remind you that special discounts are available to members of the T.J. O'Shaunessy's Good-Time Grub Club! Can I start you off with some drinks?"

The old man in a tweed jacket ordered a Scotch. The middle-aged man in a sportcoat and tie ordered a beer. The young man in a polo shirt and khakis ordered a soda.

The waitress asked them if they were attending the rare book conference, which they confirmed. She told them they were eligible for a discount, left them menus, cleared the place setting in front of the unused fourth chair at their table and left.

The three men once again turned their attention to the book, bound in what appeared to be worn, cracked leather. It hung on the wall next to their table, flanked by an old tin Coca Cola sign and a Rosemary Clooney album cover.

"I really don't think it's anything," the young man said. "These places just throw a bunch of antique crap up on the walls for decoration."

"Yeah," the middle-aged man said. "Seems like a coincidence that it would show up at the same conference center where a bunch of rare book dealers are meeting."

"Precisely," the old man said. "It is not a coincidence at all. The book has a way of finding those who might use it. Or, should I say, those whom it might use."

The waitress returned with their drinks.

"I'd like to tell you about our specials," she said. "The soup of the day is bacon bisque. Dinner special is Cajun fried cheesesteak poppers with three sides and T.J. O'Shaunessy's world-famous all-you-can-eat potato bar. And from 5 to 7, Frozen Tequila Fanny Bangers are a dollar. I'll give you a few more minutes."

They thanked her and she left. The old man's voice dropped to a harsh whisper as he eyed the other two from beneath bristling, white eyebrows.

"I tell you, it's no mere chain restaurant wall decoration," the old man said. "It is the Grimoire of Darkness. Bound in human flesh. Written in human blood, in the language of an ancient, long forgotten race rumored to be something other than human."

"Really?" the young man said. "You think it might be worth something?"

He reached out to run his fingers over the binding.

"No, you fool!" the old man cried, jumping to his feet and knocking his chair over backwards.

But the young man's features had already slackened into a dazed expression. He seemed in a trance as he stood, removed the book from the wall and opened it. The waitress hurried over.

"Sir, you can't …" she began, but stopped when the young man scowled at her and bellowed in a deep voice not his own.

"Silence, mortal!"

In the same strange, deep voice, the young man began to read from the book. The lights dimmed and an unearthly chill permeated the restaurant while his mouth emitted incomprehensible, guttural syllables. A black mass coalesced around the empty chair, and materialized into corporeal shape.

The thing that reposed in the chair was an abomination of writhing tentacles dripping with fetid ichor, the pale color of something long dead. About its monstrous form clacked a profusion of mandibles, and shone clusters of black orbs that resembled eyes but on closer inspection appeared to be portals into boundless depths of blackness beyond which alien constellations burned in arcane configurations. Its very mass seemed to pulsate in and out of being, as though occupying an alien geometry beyond the capacity of three dimensions to accommodate or human mind to grasp.

When the thing spoke, its voice was a chill wind blowing from spaces beyond knowing. A multitude of whispers. A chorus of madness.

"If I can make a suggestion," it said, "try the curly fries."

A DARK STORMY NIGHT

A dark stormy night is cliché

But the evening had started that way

A knife and a gun

And some poison for fun

That makes up for the first line, okay?

A HOMELESS HAUNTING
Michael J. Clarke

Frustrated by hissing air and static crackle from the car radio, Fred Elwood stopped fiddling with the dial and slammed his fist against the dashboard.

"Damned this used car! Dysfunctional just like my life since the divorce. Why do I bother? I should just drive across the center line and end it."

He was seconds away from a tearful breakdown, when a strange voice interrupted his dispirited soliloquy.

"Seems rather extreme, doesn't it? Want to think it over?"

Fred didn't believe in haunted cars, and never expected to own one. Yet the cadaverous man seated next to him was certainly a ghost. Fred could see right through him.

"I died in this car," said the ghostly man. "I was murdered in the back seat."

Fred was uncomfortable. "Uh ... sorry to hear that," he said.

"Thanks! You're the first person to talk to me. Everybody else leaves when I say that. Don't you want to get away from me?"

Fred couldn't control the shaking. He kept his hands firmly clamped on the steering wheel, with eyes fixed straight ahead on the highway. He avoided looking to his right as he answered, in a frightened voice. "If I wasn't stuck in traffic in the middle lane of I-95, I'd pull over and run!"

"I wouldn't want you to do that. You might have an accident." The ghost was sincerely anxious. "What can I do to help calm you down?"

"Leave! Can't you just float away?"

"Sorry. Not possible. My ectoplasmic self is anchored to your engine."

"Your what?"

"Oh, sorry. Ghost talk. It's that misty, viscous stuff that has to steam off before I can manifest. Mediums are good at bringing it out through a spiritualistic trance. It's one of the first things ghosts learn to do. Good thing, too. Not much chance of finding a medium in this place, is there?"

"Uh . . . no. I guess not."

"Right. Feeling better now?"

"Could you maybe move into the trunk? I'd be more comfortable driving in traffic if you weren't looking at me."

"Oh, I don't know if I want to do that. It's really uncomfortable back there. Also, that's where the murderer put my corpse."

Fred's ears got warm. Sweat broke out on his forehead. Still not looking at the ghost, he said: "This really stinks. I can't afford to buy a new car, not on my salary. I'm going to take this heap back to the dealer and ask for a refund. Right after work."

"Hey, you look a little red in the face. High blood pressure isn't good for you. I used to take deep breaths and hold them until I could feel my body calming down. You should try that."

The ghost's soothing manner was helping take the edge off. Fred had been expecting to be threatened or scared into a heart attack. "I really need this job. I just started a few weeks ago and can't miss any days."

"You don't have to take care of it today. I've got time."

"Are all ghosts as friendly as you?"

"I wouldn't know. I'm new to this."

"Work is still twenty minutes away. So, we might as well talk. I'm Fred Elwood."

"Mason."

"Mason what?"

"I just go by Mason. I was a 'homeless guy' before my murder. Don't want to use my last name and hurt the family's reputation. I made a mistake and found myself alone on the streets."

"We have something in common." Fred felt bold enough to glance over at Mason, and quickly turned his eyes back to the road. "I made a mistake too. I married the wrong woman. She hired a shrewd lawyer who coached her on a fake story, divorced me for 'cruel and inhuman treatment' and took everything - - the house, the boat, the cars, the bank accounts. I lost a good job. Her father was my boss. I could easily have ended up sleeping on the streets like you."

"Oh, I'm so sorry. At least you kept it together. You seem to be on the road to recovery."

"If you want to call this living."

"It beats my gig."

"Ah," Fred chuckled. "Guess it does. Sorry about that, my friend."

"No need to apologize. I'm glad to have someone to talk to."

"Y'know, for a ghost, you're not so bad," Fred said. "It feels like I'm talking to a normal person."

"I am a normal person. I just became a ghost. It's not as if I made a career choice," Mason answered. "When it happened, I was just as frightened as any person would be."

"How did it happen to you?"

"I upset the wrong man. He killed me."

"Seems like a pretty extreme reaction."

Traffic was backing up, so Fred glanced over. Mason was looking back and grinning. This time Fred controlled his anxiety. Even though he could see through Mason, he could pick up some details. Younger than Fred. Maybe late twenties. Needs a haircut and shave. Wrinkled plaid lumberjack shirt. Worn blue jeans with thread-bare areas at both knees. Looks like bone showing through the holes.

Fred managed a dry swallow, and grinned back. "You look okay, for a ghost."

"And you look like a guy who's had too many meals at fast food restaurants. That's not healthy. I should know. When I have money, that's where I eat. I'd look like that, getting pudgy and jowly like you, if I ate there more often."

"You still eat? Need me to stop at a drive-thru window?"

"Oops. My bad. When I used to eat. I'm still not totally used to this ghostly form."

"That's okay. You're right. Everything you said was true. I hate leaving work and making dinner for one. I got into the habit of bringing take-out back to the apartment. Can't afford to spend much. And it's made me lazy."

"I hear you, brother. Hey, y'know something? If I got a haircut and cleaned up, and you lost some weight . . . we'd almost look like each other. Same dark hair. Similar nose. You could pass as my older brother."

Fred smiled. "Can we get back to your story? What exactly did you do that ended in death?"

"I didn't do anything to him. I just wanted to stay warm. That enraged him. He flipped out and murdered me."

"Who?"

"Jasper Geist. The owner of Friendly Motors, where you bought this car."

"Did you sneak into his house to sleep? Or break in?"

"What part of 'homeless' don't you get?"

"Oh. Right. Sorry about that."

"That's okay. I had just wandered into the North Wilmington suburbs. I was sleeping under some trees in the community park. I had to move out of the city. Homeless people have to keep moving. Find a good spot to sleep, only until some 'concerned citizen' gets bothered about it. Then the cops wake you up with a nightstick in the ribs."

"That's terrible. You can sleep at my place. I don't mind."

"Thanks for the offer. I'm sort of planted here. Your car works fine."

"Mason, when you first appeared I thought I was going crazy. But I think I'm getting used to this. I'm beginning to understand there is more than one way to define the word homeless."

"Thanks, man. I'm happy we're getting along. Anyway, I left the park and started heading south towards the city. It was getting really cold and windy, and I started shivering so hard my teeth rattled. Then, I came across the Friendly Motors car lot. I started checking car doors, and this car, the first one I tried, was unlocked. At least the lot was chained and padlocked, so nobody could hot wire a car and drive away. I crawled into the back seat and shut the door."

"And he killed you for that?"

"Yup. I knew I should've moved out of the car at sunrise. Shop owners hate it when we sleep in the front entrance of their stores. I've been kicked in the ribs so many times there are shoe-sized depressions in my bones. And here I was, sleeping on his merchandise and getting it dirty. But it was so comfortable in the car, and still cold outside. I kept closing my eyes and falling asleep."

Fred frowned, disturbed by what anger does to some people. "Seems like it would be easier to wake you up and tell you to move, or just pull you out of his car."

Mason reached out to pat Fred on the back, but his hand passed through him. "Oh, he woke me up all right. I felt a pain and opened my eyes to see him kneeling on my stomach. Before I could plead or say anything, his big hands were around my neck. I couldn't free my arms to defend myself. They went numb."

Fred clicked on the car's turn signal, and maneuvered over into the right lane, getting ready to access the exit ramp. "Choked to death. What an awful way to go."

"I know. I never realized how slow and painful it is. Your air passage closes off. Your vision starts to fade and funnels down to a pinpoint before everything goes black."

"Was it like a tunnel? Did you see your family members at the end? Did they tell you not to worry because everybody is together now?"

"Yeah, I heard those stories too. As things were turning pitch black, the only person I saw was my instructor."

"Your what?" Fred was concentrating on turning down the correct street to get to his job.

"My teacher. Where do you think the term 'spirit guide' came from, anyway?"

"What was his name?"

"Her name," Mason corrected. "I was scolded when I asked. She told me spirits have no name in the ether. That's a human construct."

"Interesting. So, when you get to the ether you lose your name and start over. Doesn't sound too bad. A change might be good for you."

"Look here, Fred. It's not that simple. She laid down the rules for me. Said I would experience a lifeless period of a few days until I became ghostly. I didn't wake up until the first time a customer started the car. I think I screamed as much as he did."

"Rules?"

"Yeah. Rules. Human beings are never free of them. Even death doesn't make them go away."

"Oh, crap. How disappointing. How many rules are there?"

"Well, just a few. It's a bit simpler than working for a living. The first rule is unbreakable. Since I was murdered in the back seat, I'm spiritually anchored to the car and in charge of haunting it. Doesn't matter where the car goes, or how many owners it has. The car remains in my 'possession'. Ha! Ghost joke."

Fred laughed at that. "Glad to see you retained your sense of humor."

"Better believe it. If you can't laugh at things, you might as well die."

"Mason, is it getting cold in here? I feel chilly. Should I turn the heat on?"

"Nope. That's just me. It's another ghost thing. Cold just seems to follow us around. Like a cheap aftershave. You get used to it. Are we at your workplace?"

"This is it. Not much, but I manage." Fred pulled into a parking spot, on a pad of cracked asphalt with spaces for approximately thirty cars. A few dandelions sprouted up through the faded lines of yellow traffic paint. The three-story office building was mostly windows on this side, gray and milky glass in need of a cleaning service. The stainless steel framework was dirty and butted up against painted concrete panels, dull and faded.

"You work here? Looks like a building in need of a good haunting."

"Not any better on the inside, but who cares? It's been vacant for a long time, so my employer enjoys cheap rent."

"So, what do you do for a living?"

"Telemarketer for home security systems. Cold-calling to set up appointments for salesmen to give estimates. Get a bonus payment if they make a sale."

"Sounds delightful."

"Mason, is this parking space okay? I tried to find you some shade. Heard the weather will be sunny and hot today."

"No problem. I stay at one temperature day and night."

"Right. That reminds me of something. Don't ghosts come out only at night? Why can I see you now?"

"That rule doesn't apply to me. Just ghosts that inhabit buildings or old battlefields. They only work midnight to 2 a.m. In my case, as soon as the engine kicks over I start up. Just takes me a few minutes to materialize."

"Why didn't I see you when I took this car for a test drive?"

"You never looked my way. If you remember, you just kept making left turns, drove around the block, and back into the lot."

"Yeah, I was afraid if I didn't act fast I would lose my chance to buy the car. It was the only one I could afford."

"More like shifty Jasper was working faster to sell it to you. All the other customers took a test drive, saw me, and drove right back.

They left in a hurry. He never got a chance to show them another car."

"It's not every day you can find a 2004 Mazda sedan for $1,500. Guess it may be the first and last one that I own. What were those other rules?"

"Well, because I died a violent death my spirit remains on this plane of existence. It can't be freed until my killer is brought to justice. I was told not to get my hopes up. The T.T.B.S.S, Transcendental Tracking Bureau of Spiritual Statistics, states that only 1 in 10,000 ghosts get closure."

"That really stinks."

"Yep. Only one more rule to remember: no howling, shrieking or moaning. I was told that over the last fifty years or so, ghosts have gotten much more benevolent, going for a kinder, gentler image."

"Guess I should've married a ghost. Your folk seem more civilized than we flesh and blood mortals."

"Maybe, I guess." Mason was still smiling, with a big openmouthed grin. It looked a little creepy that instead of seeing his teeth, Fred was viewing the passenger side door. "I don't want you to be late for work. You need to get going. I'll be right here, taking a nap."

#

By mid-morning, Fred was ready to call it a day. His phone conversations lacked zip and enthusiasm. Even though he had a printed script in front of him with several suggested responses to various questions, he had trouble focusing and staying on task. He failed to make a single appointment for the sales reps. His thoughts kept returning to Mason, as he searched for ways to help him free his spirit.

Fred thought of going to the police to report the murder. And when they asked for proof, should he reply that a ghost told him? Too far-fetched, wouldn't be taken seriously. Needs solid evidence. Too bad the police can't be taken to the burial site. Mason was still in the 'recovery room' when that happened, so he doesn't know where to look. It's going to require a confession from Mr. Geist.

Fred came up with a vague plan. He feigned sickness and was permitted to end his workday after the lunch breaks were finished.

When he reached the parking lot and entered his car, he noticed the absence of Mason. He called his name but received no reply.

"Mason needs closure, and deserves it," he proclaimed to the front seat. "I'm going through with this. I've been leading a meaningless life lately and now I have purpose."

Fred put the key in the ignition and started the car. After backing out and driving away from the parking lot, he sensed the presence of a companion. Mason had reappeared in the passenger seat, a little faint at first but clearer now.

Mason yawned. "That was a shorter nap than I expected. Where are we going? Out for lunch today?"

"Lunch is over. I was excused from work early. We're going back to Friendly Motors to finish your business with Jasper Geist."

\#

From the window of his office trailer, Jasper Geist saw the familiar Mazda pull into the dusty lot. For a beefy man, he moved swiftly. He walked to his executive desk and sat down, facing the door. He heard the footsteps on the wooden ramp to the trailer entrance, followed by a knock. Jasper reached inside his desk drawer before replying. "Come in."

Fred's left hand was in his pocket, fumbling with his cell phone. "Hello, Mr. Geist. I'm Fred Elwood. I bought a used Mazda from you yesterday."

"Right, right. Mr. Elwood. How's the car treating you? Happy with it? You've got a real deal there."

"I want to return it for a full refund."

"Something wrong with the car?"

"Yes, something that can't be fixed. It's haunted by a ghost."

"Ha!" Geist put his right arm up in the air and jabbed a finger at Fred. "I thought I heard every reason a customer could think of for bringing a car back. But I never heard that one before. A ghost! You didn't happen to see a pink elephant in there as well, now did you?"

"You're not funny. I want you to take the car back." Now it was Fred's turn to jab a finger. "And return every cent that I paid for it."

"I don't care about your phony story. You seem to have forgotten the details in the sales contract. You signed and agreed to buy the car 'as is'. The buyer takes on all responsibility for the car after purchase. The sale is final. You are stuck with it and whatever problems it has."

"Stop acting innocent, Mr. Geist." Fred's ears began to warm up again, this time from rage. He walked up to the desk and thumped it with his fists. "You know what happened. The ghost told me. You murdered him."

Geist jumped back. "That's the craziest thing I've ever heard."

"Wrong. Things have never been clearer. And I know you did it. Your body language just gave you away."

Geist stood up, face red with anger, mirroring Fred's color. "What's one less hobo on the streets going to matter? I probably did that degenerate a favor, putting him out of his misery."

"His name is Mason. He deserves your respect. How could you do something like that?"

Geist sat back down, working to compose himself as well as calm down his accuser. "I didn't mean to do it. I'm actually a kind, considerate person." A weak smile for Fred's benefit. "You just don't know the kind of pressure I'm under. The night before I had to leave work early to meet my probation officer. I had a late customer, so I didn't have time to make sure all the cars were locked up." Geist bowed his head now and put on his best remorseful look. "When I found him the next morning sleeping in the car, I just lost it. I'd take it back if I could. This has been bothering me for a long time."

"What did you do with the body?" Fred asked.

"At first, I moved it to the trunk. I was going to bury it in the park. But I decided to dig a hole and bury it underneath the office trailer, where I could make sure nobody would find it."

"It's a little late for you to be feeling sorry. It's too late for Mason."

Geist extended his hand towards Fred, as if to complete a handshake. "What if I gave you half your money back? And, you can keep the car."

Fred's stern reply was "No deal. You've told me what I need to know. I'm taking this information to the police." He backed towards the door, preparing to leave.

Geist reached underneath his desk and stood quickly, waving a hand gun. "You're not going anywhere."

Fred had no time to react. He felt an explosion of pain in his knee. He went down hard on the trailer floor and desperately tried to scramble away.

Geist followed closely behind Fred, who managed to crawl down the trailer ramp and drag himself across the gravel towards the car.

"You should've taken the deal. I did time in jail. My probation officer was bribing me. I had to kill him. A detective was just here asking questions about his disappearance. I can't let you go to the police. This business is all I have left." He moved the gun closer, ready to place it against Fred's temple.

"Wait." Fred raised his arm, putting his hand in front of the gun. "If I'm going to die, I'm not haunting a parking lot." He backed into the Mazda and laid down on the back seat. "This way Mason will have a companion."

"As you wish, you sicko." Geist reached to the floor of the back seat, grabbed Fred's emergency blanket and threw it at him. "Wrap that around your head. I need to keep the car clean for the next buyer." Nervous laugh. "I don't see a ghost here. Looks like your friend has skipped town, dumb ass."

Fred didn't bother to explain. He also didn't tell Geist about the two phone calls he made before leaving from work. One to the police precinct, and one to the local television station. He told them that Jasper Geist was a murderer of homeless people. He would prove it and supply them with evidence. Fred had a confession recorded on his cell phone. If they came to Friendly Motors at approximately 2:45 p.m., they would find the bodies.

Instead of speaking to Geist, Fred addressed Mason. "Justice is coming, my friend! After we get to the ether, we need to look each other up and have a drink."

FEMME FATALE
Tony Conaway

It's tough being a narcoleptic. If I don't take my meds, I'm liable to pass out at any time.

And when you look like me, that means you're liable to wake up with some scumbag on top of you.

Even before I opened my eyes, I knew two small hands were feeling me up. I slowly reached around and got a grip on the revolver that I holster in the back of my bodice.

I opened my eyes, pulled out my pistol, and aimed it down at his face. "Move and you're dead, little man."

He kept grinning. He was happy to freeze with his hands on my breasts. Me, I just wanted to get some distance between us so he couldn't slap the gun out of my hands.

I scooted away on my backside until I was out of his reach. He didn't seem to recognize me. Well, it had been years since we last met. "You're the one they call Lust," I said.

He remained in his crouch and let out a lewd whistle. Big whistlers, these seven Vice Brothers – just as I recalled.

"Where are the other six?"

He stopped whistling and licked his lips. "I may be small, but I'm all the man you need, baby."

"Don't call me *baby,*" I said. "The name is White. *Snow* White." And I shot him twice, once in each knee.

While he moaned and tried to keep from bleeding out, I stood and walked to a safer position. I kept my back to the mountain and looked around, but no one seemed to be coming to his aid.

"I'll ask you again: where are your brothers?"

"Ahhh, I dunno. Greed and Gluttony are in the mine, and Sloth is probably sleeping somewhere. I don't know about the others. Ahhh, it hurts!"

I didn't think I'd get anything else useful out of him, so I double tapped him. One in the head, one in the heart.

And dammit, I got a splash of his blood in my cleavage after all.

#

After I wiped the blood off, I took out my pill bottle and popped another amphetamine. Yup, that's what they give you for narcolepsy – speed. I couldn't risk falling asleep on the job again.

Obviously, health care doesn't come with my unofficial job as assassin-for-hire. I'm technically a consultant for Ms. Queen, our semi-deranged Commander-in-Chief. Just a few years ago, she became insanely jealous of my looks. Some *Mirror* poll said I'd surpassed her as "the fairest in the land." I suspect she's the one who tried to poison me right around then. I survived, but that's when my narcolepsy began.

Fortunately, I convinced Ms. Queen that "fairest in the land" was bull – sorry, I forgot that I gave up swearing for Lent. It's a *nonsensical* title. People have different standards of beauty. Some men like tall woman, some men like them curvy. We did a quick *Screw-Marry-Kill* poll over the internet. I won *Screw,* she won *Marry.* Oh, and my homicidal sister Rose won *Kill.* Rose scares people.

Over a few bottles of wine, we finally agreed that Ms. Queen was the hottest *blonde* in the land, while I was the hottest *brunette.* And that was that. I went back to killing men (and getting paid for it), while Queenie went back to staying up half the night and sending out misspelled Tweets.

My latest contract was to terminate these seven dwarves. They've gone by a lot of names, but "the Vice Brothers" describes them perfectly. Ms. Queen personally ordered the hit. She decided they're a bad influence on children. I had my own history with them, and I couldn't agree more.

I reloaded my gun and adjusted my bodice. Hey, I didn't ask to be born beautiful. I just use what I've got. And since men usually stare at my décolleté, that gives me more time to shoot them.

The dwarves lived in a cabin to the east; the mine entrance was to the west. West was closer, so I headed that way.

As I neared the entrance, I found Sloth sleeping on a rock outcrop in a warm sunbeam. He never woke up. Don't judge me -- there are a worse ways to go than in your sleep. Considering the profession I'm in, I doubt I'll be that lucky.

Two dwarves down, five to go.

I paused at the mine entrance. I could hear two voices inside, getting closer. Peering inside, I could dimly see two dwarves, each one pushing an overloaded cart full of ore. I guessed the thin one was Greed, while the fat one with a sandwich in his mouth was Gluttony. "They all went home for lunch a half-hour ago," the latter mumbled through his sandwich. "Why do *they* get to leave early?"

I was in a good position, right outside the mine entrance. Their eyes would be blinded by the bright sunlight.

Their voices told me when they were almost at the entrance. That's when I stepped into position and fired four shots. A moment later there were two more dead dwarves. Four down, three to go.

I decided to take Gluttony at his word. Rather than search the mine for more dwarves, I headed back to their house.

#

At their rustic cabin, I heard voices from inside. The wall with the chimney lacked windows, so that covered my approach. I peeked around the corner at the open front door. I had to assume the cabin had a back door as well.

"It's not fair," came a whiny voice from inside.

"Look," said another voice. "When I cook, you clean up. Now take out the trash."

As the first voice continued to whine, I considered the situation. It sounded like the whiner would be coming outside with the rubbish. That would be the perfect time to kill him, while his hands were full. But if I used my revolver, I'd alert the one or two dwarves still inside. I didn't want them hustling out the hypothetical back door – or worse, coming out the front door with a weapon.

They had a pile of firewood next to the cabin. The axe they used to chop the wood was stuck in a stump. I pulled out the axe and got into position.

Soon, the whiny dwarf emerged with a bag of trash in each hand, muttering. This could only be the one called Envy. I waited until he crossed in front of me and brained him from behind with the axe.

That's when my luck failed. Envy fell to the ground, mortally wounded, but not yet dead. A cry came out of his mouth, followed by a loud death rattle.

The noise alerted the cooking dwarf. He ran out of the house, screaming curses at me. Wrath was surprisingly fast on his stumpy legs.

Fortunately, he hadn't stopped to grab a good weapon. All he had was his meat cleaver, raised high. I pulled out my gun and cut him down before he got near me.

Six down, one to go. But if the last dwarf was nearby, he now knew I was hunting him. Cautiously, I circled the cabin, looking in windows. The place seemed to be empty, and there was no back door. Where was he?

I soon found out. "Drop the gun," came a voice from behind me. I paused, then a shotgun blast kicked up dirt to my left. I dropped my gun. "Raise your hands and turn around," said the voice. I complied. The last dwarf, Pride, stood there, aiming a shotgun at me. Two dead rabbits lay at his feet. I guessed he'd just returned home from hunting.

Pride stood tall (for a little person), acting like the hero in a movie Western. So, of course, he had to make a speech before he killed me. "I found the corpses of Lust and Sloth. This is for my brothers. For Envy. For Wrath. And for - "

Just before he got to the end of his speech, Pride's head exploded. When my ears stopped ringing, I heard a familiar giggle from behind him.

"Good thing you asked me to watch your back," said my crazy sister. They don't call her "Rose Red" because of her hair color.

She's got brown locks, the color of mud. They call her "Red" because she's so often covered in blood.

"Well," I said, "with the odds seven-to-one, I figured I could use some backup." This time I was the one covered in blood and brain matter. Rose had blown Pride apart with her own shotgun. I scraped a gobbet of something off my face.

"Mmmm," observed Rose. "Tasty!" She picked up the brace of dead bunnies and started playing with them. "Gee, Flopsy," Rose said in a little voice. "You don't look at all well." Then she wiggled the other rabbit, which had one ear blown off. "That's right, Mopsy," Rose squeaked in a different voice. "But I still look better than that dwarf who shot us!"

I was suddenly tired again. "OK," I said. No use arguing with a crazy person. "I'm going into the cabin to find a towel. And maybe take a nap."

AFTERWARD
Tony Conaway

Technically, a *noir* story (or film) doesn't have to involve murder. Classic noir involves a crime, of course, usually perpetrated by a member of the underclass. Often, the perpetrator is a man duped by a seductive female. And it always ends badly for the perpetrator.

We've chosen to define *noir* more loosely. In our stories, the perpetrator can be female. And, since these stories were designed to take no more than seven minutes to read, there may not be time for a traditional bad ending. (Although some of the stories which appear in this volume may be longer, "expanded" versions.)

For example, the crimes in Tony Knighton's excellent story, "As Long As You Can," are phone scams. And no one has to coerce the protagonist, Hank, into a life of crime. There's no murder...although Hank's unpleasant fate is left to the reader's imagination.

The protagonist in "Overdue," the story by Joanette McGeoch, is a librarian. That's about as far as you can get from the traditional *noir* protagonist. Librarians are part of the *intelligentsia,* not the *lumpenproletariat*.

And the assassin in my story, "Femme Fatale," is straight out of a storybook.

So forgive us if we've expanded the definition of noir. It's all in the service of good, nasty stories. Enjoy.

ACKNOWLEDGEMENTS

Thank you, Jay Kennedy for suggesting the event, working through the details in Oxford and filling the many audience seats.

Thanks to **the Oxford Library** for wanting to host the event and filling the room with an audience for the great authors.

Many thanks to the **Octoraro Hotel (OTE)** for being such great hosts to the event and friends of the library.

Tony Conaway is always a go-to person for opinions, thoughts, smart observations and information on writing, people and holding events. He is the core of most writer groups in the area.

Each of the authors involved donated their skill and time to offer a story and present it. Realize that many authors would rather have root canals than have to read in public, so this is no small offering. Some even drove a significant distance to endure that discomfort. They also donated the proceeds from the book to the library.

These generous authors include: **Sarah Cain, Mike Clarke, Tony Conaway, Matty Dalrymple, Tom Joyce, Jay Kennedy, Tony Knighton, Lanny Larcinese, Walter Lawn, Matthew McGeehin, Joanette McGeoch, Scott Pruden,** and **Gary Zenker.**

Thank you to Michael Clarke who did proofreading of the final volume *twice*!

And a big thank you to our audience, for supporting the event and the library.

BIOGRAPHIES

CHRIS BAUER is author of the new political/crime thriller JANE'S BABY from Intrigue Publishing, which fictionally addresses the "what if" question of whatever happened to Jane Roe's baby of *Roe v Wade* landmark Supreme Court case fame. He's also the author of SCARS ON THE FACE OF GOD, runner up for EPIC Awards' best in ebook horror in 2010.

His short stories have been published/podcasted by *Thuglit, Shroud Magazine,* and *Well Told Tales.* Chris wouldn't trade his Northeast Philadelphia upbringing of street sports played on blacktop and concrete, fistfights, brick and stone row houses, and twelve years of well-intentioned Catholic school discipline for a Philadelphia minute (think New York minute but more fickle and less forgiving). He now lives in Doylestown, PA and still does all his own stunts, and once passed for Chip Douglas of *My Three Sons* TV fame on a Wildwood, NJ boardwalk. He likes the pie better than the turkey.

SARAH CAIN wrote her first story when she was four and has been at it ever since. A graduate of Smith College with a B. A in English, Sarah worked as a copywriter, speechwriter, and a scriptwriter. She moved onto flash fiction and then published two novels: The Eighth Circle and One By One, a pair of thrillers published by Crooked Lane Books. She is busy at work on her third novel. Married to an ex-political consultant, she is the mother of three wonderful children and one lunatic cat.

MICHAEL J. CLARKE has lived in Oxford, PA since 2000. After 40 years in the paint business, the last 17 years in field research, he retired. He now occupies his time with writing pursuits and other activities. Born in the 50's, with his formative years occurring in the '60's. His inner child never took the training wheels off. Loves all genres of pop culture. Currently hiding in Southeastern PA with family and pretending to act normal.

TONY CONAWAY has been a published writer for over twenty years. He has co-written or ghostwritten business books published by large publishing houses, including McGraw-Hill, Macmillan, and Prentice Hall. His fiction has appeared in nine anthologies and numerous publications, including *Blue Lake Review, Close to the Knuckle, Danse Macabre, Rind Literary Magazine, the Rusty Nail,* and *Typehouse Literary Magazine.*

Some of his odder credits include co-writing the script for a planetarium show and selling jokes to Jay Leno for *The Tonight Show.* He has a blog that features interviews with other authors at http://wayneaconaway.blogspot.com/

MATTY DALRYMPLE is the author of the Ann Kinnear Suspense Novels *The Sense of Death* and *The Sense of Reckoning,* the Ann Kinnear Suspense Shorts, including *Close These Eyes* and *May Violets Spring,* and the Lizzy Ballard Thrillers *Rock Paper Scissors* and *Snakes and Ladders.* Matty lives with her husband and their three dogs in Chester County, Pennsylvania, which is the setting for much of the action in *The Sense of Death* and *Rock Paper Scissors.* They enjoy vacationing on Mt. Desert Island, Maine, where *The Sense of Reckoning* takes place, and Sedona, Arizona, the setting for much of *Snakes and Ladders.*

Matty is a member of Mystery Writers of America, Sisters in Crime, International Thriller Writers, and the Brandywine Valley Writers Group.

TOM JOYCE's debut novel, "The Freak Foundation Operative's Report," was published in 2013, and his short story collection, "The Devil's Kazoo Band Don't Take Requests," came out in 2016. He's had short stories published in "Needle: A Magazine of Noir," and "Space and Time Magazine."

JAY KENNEDY is a reader, not a writer, although he did have an eighth grade essay published in two Wisconsin newspapers 48 years ago. This is his first story written since then. He is the grandfather of 3 granddaughters, 4 dogs, 5 cats, and a pig. He lives in Oxford, PA with his wife and 6 cats. He thanks everyone for their support of The Oxford Library.

TONY KNIGHTON Tony Knighton is both an author and a lieutenant in the Philadelphia Fire Department, a thirty year veteran. Born in western Pennsylvania near Pittsburgh, his family moved to Philadelphia when he was seven. With the exceptions of a short stay in Toronto, Ontario, and the military, he's been in Philadelphia ever since. Tony published the novella and story collection Happy Hour and Other Philadelphia Cruelties with Crime Wave Press. His story "The Scavengers" is included in the anthology Shocklines: Fresh Voices in Terror, published by Cemetery Dance, and his story "Sunrise" is included in the anthology Equilibrium Overturned, published by Grey Matter Press. He has also published short fiction in Static Movement Online and Dark Reveries.

LANNY LARCINESE has been writing crime fiction and non-fiction for seven years after a long work life in the corporate and entrepreneurial world. His short work has won four local prizes, and his debut crime novel, "I Detest All My Sins" is scheduled for release in September under the auspices of Intrigue Publications. His reading tonight is an excerpt from that novel. He has written two other novel-length books, currently under submission.

He is a self-proclaimed city guy, having lived in Detroit, Chicago, Boston, Hartford, and Philadelphia---in each case living right in town. The myriad experiences and vagaries of city life inform much of his fiction and other writing. His work-in-progress is a fictional account of Philadelphia's MOVE conflagration of 1985, tentatively titled, "Fire in the Belly."

When not writing--which is seldom--he and his companion and muse, Jackie Perskie, dine out, drink, gossip, talk about her painting and his writing, and the fulfillment of living the creative life.

WALTER LAWN writes poetry and short fiction. His work has been published in Every Day Fiction, River Poets Journal, and the anthology *Unclaimed Baggage*. Walter is a disaster recovery planner who lives outside of Philadelphia.

MATT McGEEHIN is an office manager and budding mystery novelist. He's lived up and down the East Coast, and has been writing for over ten years. While mystery writing is his favorite, he's known to write pieces of all genres, from children's stories to adult. Outside of writing, Matt enjoys skydiving, weightlifting, and telling terrible jokes.

JOANETTE McGEOCH has written and told many as-of-yet unpublished stories, mostly fiction. She has no desire to write a great American novel, only wants to give readers a bit of fun, an escape from every day cares and a few smiles. And to see her name on books.

Currently living in Chester County, she spends way too much time researching ancient civilizations and other curious things. Joanette is a member of the Wilmington-Chadds Ford Writers and Brandywine Writers Groups whose members continually inspire and encourage her to continue writing.

SCOTT PRUDEN is a freelance writer and former newspaper journalist whose first novel, *Immaculate Deception*, was published by Codorus Press in 2010. A West Chester resident for more than 15 years, he spend much of his youth and early adulthood in South Carolina, where many of his stories are set. He's currently at work on his second novel, *Mystery White Boy*, the first in a series following the odd and out-of-this-world adventures of small-town reporter Bond Deloach.

GARY ZENKER is a marketing strategist and implementer, with experience in a variety of industries including financial services, pharmaceuticals, health care, new home construction, architecture and more. He does a lot of writing.

Gary is also the co-founder and leader of both the Main Line Writers Group and the Wilmington-Chadds Ford Writers Group, with nearly 18 years of combined operations. The groups focus on helping members better their craft, reach their publishing goals and form relationships with other writers. His flash fiction stories have been rejected by some of the finest print and online publications in the U.S. *www.GaryZenkerStoryteller.com*

He is the author and/or editor of over 25 books including *Says Seth* and *Death Farts: More Says Seth*, co-authored with his son, and *It's Not What You Think*, his collection of Flash Fiction stories. He is also creator of WritersBloxx, a story-telling party game and writers tool. *www.WritersBloxx.com*

Gary is the architect of Noir At A Bar and publisher of this collection.

LOCAL WRITERS GROUPS

Writers of all genre and levels of experience are invited to join the area writers groups of which many of our readers are members and presenters.

The Main Line Writers Group
meets the third Monday of the month at
The Black Powder Tavern
1164 Valley Forge Rd, Wayne, PA 19087
www.MainLineWritersGroup.com

The Wilmington-Chadds Ford Writers Group
meets the second Monday of the month at
McKenzie's Brew House
451 Wilmington-West Chester Pike, Glen Mills, PA
www.Wilmington-ChaddsFordWritersGroup.com

The Brandywine Valley Writers Group
meets the third Tuesday of the month at
Ryan's Pub
124 W. Gay Street, West Chester, PA
www.BVWG.org

All meeting start at 7 pm.

Check each group's up-to-date meeting details on Meetup.com.

NOIR AT A BAR is a periodic event held to celebrate the works of local readers and offer adult audiences an evening of suspense, crime and murder.

For an updated calendar of events, please join us at: https://www.facebook.com/NoirAtABar/

We are NOT affiliated with any other Noir At The Bar events or organizations. Say we are and we'll plug ya on the spot.

A Fast Jab to the Brain

A mother with a baby in her arms robbing a convenience store. A class reunion with the high school bully. A chance encounter at a nude beach. A woman flashing her breasts at a fancy cocktail party.

What do these 37 stories have in common? There's more to the story and characters than you would first believe.

In under 1,000 words, Gary Zenker weaves fascinating tales of characters and situations that are both familiar and unusual; normal and quirky; believable and far-fetched. These are stories of love and hate; trust and betrayal; sane and outright crazy behaviors.

These stories will warm your heart, make you laugh out loud, shock your senses, and most of all make you rethink about how people relate to and interact with each other.

See more at GaryZenkerStoryteller.com

Two Danny Ryan Thrillers

From One Great
Local Author

Thrillers, Suspense Novels & Shorts by Chester County Author Matty Dalrymple

"Dalrymple's works always hang together in the most thrilling and satisfying ways."

Robert Blake Whitehill
Bestselling Author-Screenwriter
The Ben Blackshaw Series

The Devil's Kazoo Band Don't Take Requests

'Wildly imaginative and hilariously freaky.'
Michael Arnzen
Bram Stoker Award-winning author of
100 Jolts: Shockingly Short Stories

stories

tom joyce